SPECIAL MESSAGE TO READERS

THE ULVERSCROFT FOUNDATION
(registered UK charity number 264873)
was established in 1972 to provide funds for research, diagnosis and treatment of eye diseases. Examples of major projects funded by the Ulverscroft Foundation are:-

- The Children's Eye Unit at Moorfields Eye Hospital, London
- The Ulverscroft Children's Eye Unit at Great Ormond Street Hospital for Sick Children
- Funding research into eye diseases and treatment at the Department of Ophthalmology, University of Leicester
- The Ulverscroft Vision Research Group, Institute of Child Health
- Twin operating theatres at the Western Ophthalmic Hospital, London
- The Chair of Ophthalmology at the Royal Australian College of Ophthalmologists

You can help further the work of the Foundation by making a donation or leaving a legacy. Every contribution is gratefully received. If you would like to help support the Foundation or require further information, please contact:

THE ULVERSCROFT FOUNDATION
The Green, Bradgate Road, Anstey
Leicester LE7 7FU, England
Tel: (0116) 236 4325
website: www.foundation.ulverscroft.com

THE PURPLE GLOVE MURDERS

In Southern California, Gail Brevard and her law partner Conrad 'Connie' Osterlitz are relaxing at their mountain hideaway. When retired Justice Winston Craig is found dead, face down on Black Bear Lake, Gail is asked to find the cause of his death. She becomes convinced it is linked to one of his old cases. However, when Connie is attacked and lies near death, Gail must use all her resources to solve the crime before it's too late . . .

MARY WICKIZER BURGESS

THE PURPLE GLOVE MURDERS

Based on characters created
by Lionel Webb

Complete and Unabridged

LINFORD
Leicester

First published in Great Britain

First Linford Edition
published 2013

A catalogue record for this book is available
from the British Library.

ISBN 978–1–4448–1616–7

11816262

Published by
F. A. Thorpe (Publishing)
Anstey, Leicestershire

Set by Words & Graphics Ltd.
Anstey, Leicestershire
Printed and bound in Great Britain by
T. J. International Ltd., Padstow, Cornwall

This book is printed on acid-free paper

THE PURPLE GLOVE MURDERS

'Did you see this?' Connie was curled up in front of a blazing fire with the Sunday paper scattered about him, as Gail scurried about fixing coffee, orange juice, and a plate of hot spicy cinnamon buns.

'What was that?' she answered absent-mindedly, stirring a flavored creamer into her own steaming cup. Connie preferred his black. She licked the spoon and tossed it into the sink.

'Did you know a Judge Craig? Over at Black Bear? His body was discovered in the lake last night . . . '

'Oh my God, yes. He was one of Dad's oldest friends. That's terrible. Let me see . . . ' She ran to Connie's side and grabbed the paper from his hands. 'Yes, that's him. What in the world happened? Does it say . . . ?'

She scanned the article ravenously, but details were hazy. 'Apparently, he'd gone down to the lake alone to fish off the pier and fell in — but they don't seem to know exactly when — or why.' Connie scratched his head thoughtfully. 'I wonder if the old guy'd had a few snorts.'

'He did like his booze. He and Dad used to have some wild times together. But still, it seems strange that no one missed him earlier. Oh yes, here it is: 'Craig's wife had called the local hospital and sheriff's station several times throughout the evening, concerned when he didn't return' . . . '

'Hmm, well, it's certainly a tragedy. Do you want to contact the family?'

'Yes, I must. I should let Mother know, too. Let me see if I can find a number for them.' She ran off again to find her cell phone, and a short time after speaking to someone in the Craig household, she placed a call to her mother.

★ ★ ★

'I can't believe it,' Alberta Norris said. 'Win was in pretty good health the last time I saw them. Oh Lord, I think it's been at least five years ago, now. I think

4

they came back here to attend a conference or something. How's his wife taking it? It must have been a terrible shock for her.'

'I don't know anymore than I told you, Mother. Connie and I are going over there now to pay our condolences. Maybe they'll have more information by then. I'll give you a call when we get back, and try to find out when the services will be. We'll need to send flowers.'

'Yes, I'll handle that if you like. Why don't we go in together on an arrangement? I think that would be more appropriate . . . ' Alberta's voice wandered off as she pondered the social requirements.

'All right, then. Let me speak to Erle quickly.' Erle Stanley Norris was Gail's mentally challenged younger brother who still lived at home in his mother's care. Gail tried to maintain the bond with him as much as possible, even at a distance.

'Hi, Gail,' came the disconcerting deep male voice a few moments later. 'How are you? Do you have any pennies for me?' Erle loved shiny new pennies, and Gail had encouraged him to deposit them from time to time in the savings account she had established for him. His fondest hope was to save up enough to purchase a genuine magician's outfit, complete with cape and top hat ('A big black cape,' he had told her, 'with a shiny red silk lining!'; Gail had already put it at the top of her Christmas list).

'Hi Erle. Yes, I'll have a bunch of them for you when I get back. I think we'll have enough to make a deposit. Would you like that?'

'Oh yes, please! Let's do that! Make a 'posit!' Erle's voice boomed back at her in joy, already anticipating the important outing to the bank and the 'slurpy' ice cream shop treat that invariably followed. Gail, as usual, wiped away a tear or two as she disconnected from the call.

'Okay,' she said to Connie a few minutes later, grabbing a jacket and scarf. 'Let's go. I'm not looking forward to this, but I think it's something we need to do.'

★　★　★

There were at least half a dozen Mercedes-Benzes and BMWs parked in orderly fashion within the Craig compound when Gail and Connie arrived, and a courteous young man, perhaps one of the Craig grandsons, directed them to an empty space. They hurried up a wide stone walkway through the brisk September air, and were ushered in to a sitting room off the main entry. A fire blazed in one corner, and a well-stocked drinks cart sat nearby. Mrs. Craig was seated on a comfortable chintz sofa under a large plate glass window with views out toward the lake. She was surrounded by guests and family members, and a handful of servants hovered about to take food and drink orders. Several young children were at a table in the corner engrossed in a board game and sipping hot chocolate.

'What will I do? *What will I do?*' the new widow moaned, dabbing at her eyes with a soggy tissue. 'What *am* I ever going to do?'

'Please, Eva. Pull yourself together. We need to get through the funeral now. Then we'll decide what to do about all this.' The young woman speaking was, Gail knew, Winston's oldest married daughter, Joan. Eva, his second wife, was the stepmother, and Gail had never met her.

The maid who had showed them in went up to Joan and whispered in her ear. The younger woman glanced over and immediately rose to greet them. 'Gail Norris, isn't it? Please, have a seat. Thank you so much for coming. Let me introduce you to Eva.'

Gail mentioned her married name, Brevard, and introduced Connie to the two women. Eva nodded to them vaguely and motioned to one of the servants. 'Please, let them know what you'd like to drink.' Gail and Connie placed their orders and took the seats offered them nearby.

'We're so sorry for your loss. Your husband was one of my father's closest friends,' Gail began, 'and I can't imagine what you must be going through. Is there anything, anything at all, we can do to help?'

An altercation began at the children's

game table, and Joan excused herself to settle things. Eva motioned Gail a bit closer. 'You're an attorney, aren't you? A criminal lawyer? It seems to me Win mentioned something about you defending a young man successfully in a murder trial back in Cathcart. Is that true?'

Gail, somewhat surprised by the turn of the conversation, nodded her assent. 'I deal mostly in corporate matters with Connie here, but yes, occasionally I dabble in criminal law. I'm flattered that Judge Craig took note of my activities.'

'Oh, he was *very* interested. He mentioned only recently that he knew how proud Joe would have been of you and what you were doing. I think he had some thought of contacting you, to talk about the law and get your take on a few things.'

'I wish he'd done that. I would have liked that very much.' Gail paused. She had no idea what this woman, unknown to her until now, was getting at, but it seemed she had some sort of agenda. 'Was he interested in anything specific, do you know?'

'There's such a crowd here today. All these people . . . and the children . . . ' Eva raised her eyebrows as another whoop erupted from the youngsters. 'Why don't you two come back tomorrow, when things are a bit quieter. I really would like to talk with you further about all this . . . this mess.' A few more tears etched their way down her sunken cheeks, smudging her eyeliner and making a mess of their own.

Gail glanced at Connie for confirmation and he gave a slight nod. 'Of course. What time would be good for you? How about a little after ten?' They agreed on the time, then Gail rose and looked about for Joan.

After a few whispered words with Win's daughter, Gail and Connie made their way out through the gathered clan, collected their car, and drove back across the mountain toward their rented cabin. Gail gazed thoughtfully out over the cold, deep lake with its jaunty whitecaps sparkling here and there under the brilliant blue canopy overhead. She wondered what secrets might be lurking beneath its dark surface. Suddenly, a few fluffy clouds skittered by, blocking out the sun and sending them into shadow. She shook her head, trying to make sense of what had happened back at the Craig house, while Connie kept his own counsel — and his eyes on the curving road ahead of them, uncertain of what lay around the next bend.

★   ★   ★

The next day dawned crisp and clear, with a strong scent of pine in the air. An orangey-pink sun, with little or no warmth in it, hung to the east in a cobalt sky. 'Red sky in the morning, sailors take warning . . . ,' Gail sang out as she dressed casually but warmly in a dark wool pantsuit and royal blue cashmere sweater that brought out the red glints in her hair and the green in her eyes. Connie, his once-blond hair and trim beard now tinged with silver, wore his beloved blue jeans, a plaid Pendleton shirt, and a tweed sport jacket. Once they'd taken care of morning chores around the cabin, they stopped in at the local post office to check their box and pick up any mail that had accumulated over the weekend. Another quick stop for the morning paper, then on to the Apple Core, a trendy café in the tiny mountain village of Crystal Springs, where they feasted on blueberry griddle cakes smothered in butter and maple syrup, apple-flavored sausage, and tons of hot coffee. As they ate they perused their mail, discussed a few business decisions they needed to make, and looked over the local *Mountain News* with its blaring headline, 'JUDGE CRAIG DEAD!' By the time they had finished eating, it was nearly ten, and they had to rush a bit to make the fifteen-minute drive over to Black Bear.

'Come in, come in. Can I get you anything?' Eva, her tinted golden hair elegantly coifed on top of her head, was dressed in a black velour pantsuit with understated diamond studs gleaming from her ears. She greeted them in the foyer, and, turning sharply to her right, directed them into the Judge's wood-paneled office, a slightly more formal area than the cozy, chintz-flavored sitting room of the day before. Gail and Connie declined anything further to eat or drink, then took the chairs indicated in front of a lovely antique writing table that had obviously been pressed into service as a desk.

'How much have you read about Win's death?' Eva seemed more relaxed than the day before, but lines of worry creased her normally pristine forehead, and Gail noticed that her hands were shaking as she picked up a petite, flowered *demitasse* cup and took a sip.

'No more than appeared in the paper this morning.' Gail couldn't see where this was going.

'Well, the sheriff's people seem to think there was something peculiar about it all. They've called in the District Attorney's office to take a look. We'll all know more after the autopsy.'

'Autopsy? Wasn't it a straight drowning? I thought he slipped or fell into the water off the dock?' Gail was a little perplexed.

'They're telling me that any time there

is some doubt about what caused the death, they must do an autopsy.' Eva took another sip, and Gail wondered if there was something stronger in her cup. 'In any case, *I* didn't have any say in the matter. The girls, of course' — meaning Joan and her younger sister Louise — 'are furious. They're blaming *me* somehow. Why, I don't know.'

'Blaming you? For what? The autopsy? Why?'

'No! They all seem to think I was somehow to blame for his *death!*' Eva crumpled once more into tears, and Gail jumped up and went over to comfort her.

'I don't understand any of this, Eva. It seems to me that the wisest thing to do now, since it's already in process, is to wait for the autopsy and see what it tells us. Then you'll know better how to proceed.'

'Oh, thank you! I knew you would understand. Win was right about you.' Eva shuddered a little, then waved Gail back to her seat. 'Now, as to why I asked you here today . . . '

Gail sat back down and glanced at

Connie. He raised one eyebrow, and they both waited.

'I would like to retain you, you and Mr. Conrad Osterlitz here, as my attorneys, in case I should need representation.' Suddenly, Eva Craig seemed much more business-like. 'Once the autopsy comes back, I'd like you to assess the circumstances, and protect and advise me if there are any problems or questions about Win's death.' She sat back and looked at them appraisingly. 'I'm willing to advance you $50,000 from my personal funds to secure your services, if and when they are needed. You are qualified to practice in California, aren't you?'

'We are,' Gail said, but looked over at Connie in consternation. 'Surely, though . . . '

'Now, hear me out,' Eva interrupted. 'I have done nothing wrong. But I'm not stupid. And I know how quickly the tide can turn. I was brought up in Europe, and I know only too well how the authorities can get the wrong idea about things. Louise, bless her heart, is young and naïve, and would never believe ill of anyone. But Joan is neither young nor naïve, and she can be quite a conniver, that one.' Eva paused and took another delicate sip from her cup. 'Now, I have no idea how this all will resolve itself. I just want to act in advance of anything. I may be borrowing trouble, but I want to be prepared for the worse-case scenario.' She sat back, exhausted, and gazed imploringly at Gail.

'Could you excuse us for a minute or two, Eva? We really can't make a decision on this without discussing it further.' Gail looked at Connie for confirmation, and he nodded. She had no idea what he was thinking right now, but her own mind was whirling.

'Of course.' Eva rose and headed toward the door. 'I'll be waiting in the little sitting room. Join me there when you've decided.'

★　★　★

And, in the end, they agreed to act as Eva Craig's representatives. After all, Gail thought cynically, how could they turn

16

down $50,000 in cash? Connie insisted, however, that they get some sort of instructions, in writing, as to what exactly the Widow Craig was expecting from them for their retainer. 'After all,' he said laconically, 'you don't really know her all that well.'

'Hell! I don't *know* her at all!' Gail snorted. 'In fact, her maiden name could be 'Braun,' and she may have been Hitler's Girl Friday in a past existence!'

So, later that afternoon, once papers had been signed and notarized, Gail sat down at her laptop and began researching the life and times of Judge Winston Craig. 'Might as well get a head start on it,' she said, when Connie questioned the wisdom of jumping ahead when they didn't know yet what the outcome of the autopsy would be.

'After all,' he said. 'It might come back as just an accidental drowning — and that would be the end of it.'

'All the same,' she said. 'I'm curious now, and I can't for the life of me figure out what she's so antsy about. If she's done nothing wrong, as she claims,

Connie, then why in bloody Hell is there so much drama?'

* * *

But a few days later, just as the Judge's family and friends had gathered at the compound for a quickly-planned memorial service (his body still had not been released by the authorities for burial), things took a decided turn 'for the worse.' To give the officials credit, they waited in the wings until all the eulogies had been given and all the outside guests had voiced their condolences to the Judge's widow and family. Then, like great black hawks, they swooped in, and Eva's fears became a reality.

'Mrs. Eva Craig?' Captain Reynolds, the steely-eyed detective representing the District Attorney's Office, confronted her. 'I am sorry to have to inform you that I have a search warrant for these premises. I also must ask you to remain where we can question you, if necessary.'

Gail stepped forward to intervene. 'Do you have a warrant for her arrest?' And after ascertaining that no such warrant had yet been issued, Gail informed the man that her client would cooperate with the search warrant, but would under no circumstances answer any questions without representation present. Connie, after a brief consultation with the officer in charge, was allowed to tag along and monitor the search.

Eva dissolved into tears and, near collapse, let Gail lead her to a secluded corner of the house, out of the way of the general search, which had now begun in earnest. Joan and Louise were allowed to take their families to a guesthouse in another area of the compound to await further instructions. The servants were gathered in the study where a mini-command quarters had been set up, although two of them were pressed into service to make a huge run of strong coffee and plates of hearty sandwiches, both for the officers and for those required to wait. Another contingent of searchers was sent down to the lakeside, where they began to go over the dock and nearby beach, looking for, Gail thought,

'God knows what.'

Connie returned twenty minutes later with bad news. 'They've found something . . . ' he said. Eva began to moan.

'What have they found? Do you know?' Gail, notebook in hand, had been jotting down a myriad of things they would need, and motions she should seek to place at the local justice court.

'Apparently, the autopsy revealed some sort of sedative that could have made Winston woozy enough to cause the accident. Now they claim they've found traces of it hidden on the property.'

'Where on earth did they find it?'

But Gail didn't get a chance to ask any further questions. Reynolds had suddenly appeared and had stepped in front of Eva.

'Mrs. Eva Craig, you are under arrest for the murder of Judge Winston Craig . . . ' He continued on, reading her rights to her as Gail and Connie stood by.

'Remember,' Gail cautioned her client, as the uniformed officers led Eva away. 'Don't say a word until I'm present.'

Then, turning to Connie, 'What in the world did they find?'

'Is this yours?' Reynolds asked a shaken Eva. He held up what appeared to be a crumpled evening glove. 'Does this belong to you?'

'I . . . I don't . . . I don't recall.' Eva stared at the lavender-hued mound of satin in front of her.

Gail peered at the glove closely. It seemed to be of vintage cut and material, something from the 1940s or '50s, perhaps. Certainly not the sort of thing a fashion-savvy woman like Eva Craig would have in her wardrobe.

'Where did you find it?' she interrupted, watching Reynolds closely.

'I'm sorry. I'll be the one asking questions here.' He indicated the whirring tape recorder in front of them. The interrogation was being held, in Gail's presence, in a secluded room at the Black Bear Sheriff's Station. 'Mrs. Craig? You're saying you've never seen this item before?'

'She's already answered that, Detective,' Gail said. He frowned at her, but moved on.

'Are you in the habit of taking any kind of sleeping pills or tranquilizers?'

Gail nodded at her client.

'Once in awhile,' Eva said, 'if I'm having trouble sleeping — I have a prescription for something to help me relax . . . '

'We'll need your doctor's name and a copy of the prescription.'

Gail nodded again, adding a mental note to her growing list.

'Does this look familiar to you?' He held up a small sterling silver pill box, intricately etched with the letter 'C.'

'Why, yes. That's what I keep . . . kept my pills in. Next to the bed. But I lost it a few months ago. Where in the world did you find it? I didn't think I'd ever see it again. Win had it engraved for me . . . ' She looked as if she might begin crying again, but somehow her tears had all been spent.

'Do you know how many pills were left in the box when you er . . . misplaced it? How many out of the original prescription had been used?'

'No. I don't think there were very

many. A dozen maybe?'

'Well, it contained only a residue of powder when we found it — inside the glove. And the glove was stuffed into a fishing creel inside the equipment box on the dock. We're in the process of having the powder analyzed as we speak, but it appears to be the same substance that Judge Craig may have ingested before his death. We believe the quantity was sufficient to make him groggy enough to lose his balance and fall into the water.' Reynolds ticked off the points one by one. 'When was the last time *you* visited that dock?'

'Why, I don't really remember. Labor Day, I suppose. The family was all here and we had a cook-out on the beach. I don't think I've been down there since then. It's begun to turn chilly, you see . . . ' Her voice trailed off.

'I think that's all for now,' Gail broke in. 'You've asked enough questions for the time being. Mrs. Craig is obviously overwrought and needs to rest. I believe we should have her examined by her physician before we go any further with this. And just so you know, I'll be requesting her release on OR as soon as possible.'

'All right, Counselor. But just so *you* know, we'll be requesting maximum bail, under the circumstances.'

'That's preposterous! She has ties to the community. I'm sure we can have any number of good citizens vouch for her, including the family.'

'That might be a problem . . . the family, I mean. The daughters are cooperating with us. I think they just might know more than you think about all this.'

Gail frowned. This was an unexpected turn. Although, on reflection, Eva *had* warned her about Joan being a 'conniver.'

'Nevertheless, Mrs. Craig is definitely not a risk for flight, or for anything else, for that matter. Just make sure her doctor is allowed to see her. I'll call him as soon as possible. In the meantime,' she said, turning to Eva. 'Don't say anything else at all, to *anyone*. And don't worry. We'll have you out of here as quickly as we can.'

'A word, Counselor,' Reynolds said as she rose and gathered her things.

'Of course.' She moved out of the room ahead of him, then turned. 'What?'

'The daughters have said they're afraid to be around her, so they want to have a few days to get their families moved out of the main house before she returns. Just so you know. Could be a little awkward.'

'Fine,' Gail snapped. 'We'll put her up at the Lodge, if necessary. Just let me know when the 'coast is clear.' And — thanks for the heads-up.'

* * *

'God!' Gail rubbed her aching eyes and slammed the laptop shut. 'I have no idea what to do next. Any suggestions?'

'I think we better give Hugo a call. See if he can come out . . . or send someone. We're shooting in the dark, here. I don't have any more ideas than you do.'

Connie was referring to one of their old standbys, Hugo Goldthwaite. The Goldthwaites, father and son, ran one of the premier detective agencies in Gail's hometown of Cathcart, and Gail and Connie kept the firm on retainer.

'Yep, you're right. We can use all the snoop help we can get. I'll see if Jr.'s available. This is right up his alley.'

And, indeed, Hugo, Jr. was able to clear his calendar and book the next flight out. 'He'll be on the red-eye landing in Ontario tomorrow morning. I've rented a car for him to pick up. We should go over our notes and get some sort of agenda ready for him by the time he arrives. I've booked a suite at the Lodge as well. We can use it as a headquarters of sorts, as well as a crash pad for any other pros we need to bring in.' Gail hummed to herself as she set about making reservations and arrangements. 'Let's see . . . we'll need a FAX machine set up there, DSL, what else?'

'Hugo's bringing his 'sweeping' equipment, right?' Connie was referring to the phone and room sweeps the P.I. conducted at any site away from their offices (which were swept on a regular basis by the Goldthwaites).

'Oh, yes. Did you get the check

deposited all right?' One of Connie's first steps had been to set up a trust account at the local Mountain Community Bank with the $50,000 check from Eva Craig. They would more than likely have need of those funds for supplies and services over the next few weeks — or even months.

'Yeah, no problem. Apparently, she has a general account there with all sorts of savings back-ups. Interestingly, she had separate accounts from her husband's. Although that's not too unusual these days. At least it makes our task easier.'

Now that they were in the thick of things, Gail and Connie settled into work mode. They contacted their offices in Cathcart, and put all possible meetings and appointments on hold until one or the other of them could get back and play catch up. The Tucson branch was already being run by an associate, so they had no need to make adjustments there, although they did let Charles know what they were up to.

'Wow, fifty G's? That's great, guys. Wish I could be in on all the fun!' Charles Walton was a trained litigator, and loved courtroom action. Gail had first met him when she was working on the Damon Powell case, and had been impressed with his professionalism. He had jumped at the offer to run Connie's Tucson offices, and had done a stellar job ever since.

'Well, if we get in a bind, we might just take you up on that,' said Gail.

★   ★   ★

The next morning, as if to mirror the dim state of Eva's affairs, a rain squall blew through, bringing with it the end of Indian summer and the first icy inklings of fall. Gail, bundled in a heavy coat, gloves, and boots, headed over to the Lodge to check on the arrangements there and reserve a suite for Eva, should she be successful in getting her client released on her own recognizance.

A bleary-eyed Hugo, in blue jeans, and with the beginnings of a five-o'clock shadow, was already waiting for her in the lounge, sipping gratefully at a steaming mug of coffee, and reviewing several of the local newspapers which had been avidly covering 'The Purple Glove Murder,' as Craig's death was now being called.

'Want one?' he asked, gesturing to his mug.

'No, thanks. We ate early and I'm all 'coffee-ed' out for now. What do you think?' She gestured at the papers scattered about his chair.

'Well, looks pretty circumstantial to me. Other than the pill container, they don't seem to have much to connect the glove to her. Has she said anything to you?'

'She seems pretty dazed. I tried to leave her be last night. She was beat by the time Reynolds got through with her. I did contact her physician and ask him to go around. He seemed a bit reluctant, but hopefully he changed his mind. I'll know more this morning when I go in to file for the OR.'

'Any hopes of that?'

'Well, we'll see. I don't really think they have much in the way of grounds to refuse it — for now, anyway. I wish we knew more about that glove, though, and where it came from. That's where I think you should start digging. Check antique stores, consignment shops, and the like. There's a whole row of them on Main Street. See if you can find anyone who recalls anything like that. It's an unusual item, and it had to come from somewhere. And, of course, the big question is, where's the mate to it?'

'Okey-dokey, babe. I need to shower and shave. Just thought I'd touch bases with you first. Then I'll head out and see what I can turn up. I'm wondering about costume shops as well? The way it's described, it could almost be like a stripper's prop. I might nose around in some of the topless bars . . . '

'You won't find much of that around here. This is a pretty exclusive area, remember. But we're not that far from Santo Verdugo. That's got a few joints like that.'

'See ya when I see ya, then. Give me a call if anything turns up . . . and I'll do the same.' Hugo gave her a swift peck on the cheek, then headed off to his suite. Gail requested an interview with the manager and outlined her requirements

. . . 'for the duration,' she said. 'I have no idea how long we'll need all this, but I'd certainly appreciate any leeway you can give us.'

'No problem, Ms. Brevard,' Mr. Brown said. 'We're at your service.' This would be a profitable solution to the on-going recession, Ben Brown thought to himself. The longer they stayed, the better.

★   ★   ★

'Look at this, Connie!' Gail wiped her perspiring brow. It was getting a bit warm inside their cozy cabin. Perhaps they had started the fire blazing too early this afternoon. She shoved her sweater sleeves up, leaned back, and stretched. 'Whew! I think I could use some fresh air.'

'What'ya got, babe?' Connie leaned over and looked at the screen she had pulled up on her laptop. 'What in the hell . . . ?!'

Gail had been scanning various data-bases, using key words like 'purple,' 'lavender,' or 'lilac' gloves, 'evening gloves,' 'vintage gloves,' etc. She had just about given up when suddenly, there it was! A hit on the phrase 'Purple Gloves Murder Trial!'

'Well, I'll be!' Connie scratched his head in disbelief.

'What's more, guess who the defense attorney was on the case?'

'Winston Craig! I think you're on to something here. You keep reading and I'll see if I can raise Hugo.' He grabbed his phone and hit speed-dial. He listened a few minutes then spoke rapidly into the receiver. 'Just got his voice-mail. I've left him a message to call in as soon as possible.'

He returned to Gail's side, and wordlessly they scanned through the brief news article that had surfaced. 'This is from over fifty years ago! Back when Craig was still practicing law. Do any of these names ring a bell with you?'

'No, but I'm going to copy this all off.' She turned to the small printer set up on their makeshift worktable. 'I think I'll give Mother a call and see if she remembers anything about the case. Looks like it was a very brief trial, which came to a very bad end for the defendant, who ended up with a life sentence in Tehachapi. Let's see . . . her name was Elisabeta Gutman. She apparently was accused of setting fire to the house where she and her husband were staying — he was killed in the blaze. One of the pieces of evidence was — *look at this, Connie!* — A purple evening glove. And hidden in the glove was a small vial containing sleeping pills!'

Just then Connie's phone buzzed. He grabbed it and spoke to the caller, then hung up. 'That was Hugo. He has some information also, and suggested we meet him at The Pine Cone. He hasn't eaten lunch yet, and I figured you could use a little break.'

'Great! Just let me finish running this off.' They grabbed their coats and ran out the door. The Pine Cone was a bar and grill about a block down the hill from their cabin, so instead of driving, they walked. By the time they reached the restaurant and slipped into the booth Hugo was holding for them, Gail's cheeks were pink and the brisk air had refreshed her overheated brain cells.

'Look at this, Hugo,' she crowed, shoving the copied file across the table. 'What do you think?'

'And you look at this,' he echoed smugly, tossing her a shopping bag marked with the name of a local consignment shop.

Gail opened up the sack and could hardly believe her eyes. There, nestled in a mound of other clothing, was the mate to the purple glove. 'Where on earth did you find this?' she said. 'It's got to be a match!'

'The lady in the shop didn't really know much. You know, they just rent out those booths to various people, and they don't ask too many questions about what they bring in. I was rooting around in the back, and there it was, peeking out of a drawer. I couldn't believe it myself. I did get a name, though — and you're not going to like it.'

'Eva Craig?'

'You got it. She had brought in several bags full of designer gowns for consignment sale, which ended up in this particular booth. The glove, apparently, just happened to be in the mix.'

'Happened? Well, I think we'd better 'sit' on this for a while. I don't want Reynolds making the connection until we figure out what's going on. By the way, did the shop owner make much of this?'

'No, I actually don't think she knew it was there. When I spotted it, I just wadded it up with a couple of other items in the drawer, and she gave me a 'one for all' price on the bag of stuff. Want any extra scarves, nighties, or shit?' Hugo grinned at her.

'That's all right, save them for your lady friends. And good thinking. I was afraid the shop owner might have it all over the village by now. You know, 'Purple Glove Mate Shows Up'!'

'Yeah, that's what I figured. It sort of looked to me like it had just been poked into that drawer. Either by the Craig woman, or by the woman renting the space.'

Just then their lunches were served, and there was a moment of silence as they dug in to juicy burgers, fries, and ice tea.

'What *was* the name of the woman who

rented the consignment booth, by the way . . . were you able to get it?'

'*Jane Brown*, if you can believe it! Sounds like an AKA if you ask me. I was in the process of trying to track her down when I got Connie's call. I'll get back to that, unless there's something else you think would give us a better shot.'

'No, you go ahead and nose about. See what you can find out about this 'Jane Brown.' In the meantime, I need to get over to the Justice Court, and see if I can get some sort of OR motion filed. Then I need to try and talk to Eva's doctor. Connie — what are you up to this morning?'

'I'm still curious about Eva's bank accounts. I thought I'd go downtown and look about a bit in the Verdugo County Hall of Records . . . see if anything interesting turns up over the last few years. Do you know how long Eva and Winston have been married?'

'I'd have to ask Mother. I wanted to run this 'Purple Glove Murder' thing by her as well. I'll give her a call while you're settling up. I can walk over to court from here, so you can go ahead and get a head start on the drive down the hill. Hugo? Can you drop Connie off to pick up our car?'

Hugo nodded as he stuffed one last French fry into his mouth. 'Mmm, that was good. I didn't realize how hungry I was. Sure, I'll drop Connie off. You can give me a shout when you're through at the courthouse, and I'll pick you up.'

'Thanks. Now, let me see about Mother.' Gail headed off down the hall toward the ladies' room, where she refreshed her lipstick, then placed a call to Alberta Norris.

'Mother? It's me, Gail. Yes, I'm fine. I have another update on the Craig situation. First of all, I need to know how long Win and Eva were married . . . do you recall? Twenty years? That would make it about 1990 or so? And do you remember when Win's first wife died? A few years before that, you think? Thanks. Connie's going down to the Hall of Records this afternoon, and it will give him a window to research. Now, there's something else. Do you recall, about fifty or sixty years ago, that Win defended a woman in a case that the newspapers here called the 'Purple Glove Murder'?'

'Oh my! That does sound familiar!' Alberta paused. 'But I can't quite — let me see. Fixty or sixty years ago? That would be around 1950 or thereabouts? I'm sorry, Gail. It does sound vaguely familiar, but I just can't remember. I'll think about it and look through some of Joe's old scrapbooks. I'll let you know if I find anything.'

'Thanks so much, Mother. That will be very helpful. I'm in a rush, so I can't take the time to talk to Erle, but give him my love — and tell him I haven't forgotten about the pennies! Talk to you soon.'

Gail made her way back out to the restaurant lobby, where Hugo and Connie were waiting. She gave Connie the approximate date for the Craig second marriage, then thought of something else. Turning to Hugo she added: 'Why don't you see if you can also find out anything about the death of Win's first wife. Her name was Linda. It seemed to me she died of cancer or something, but I just don't recall the details right now. I'm wondering how long it was before he married again. And I'd also like to know if Eva was acquainted with Linda — or if she came on the scene later. Just curious. Now . . . let's see if I can spring our caged bird.'

★   ★   ★

'Next case,' rumbled the bailiff, 'number SV-2370692; the State of California v. Eva Elisabeth Eleanora Craig.' Gail was already seated at the front table with a disheveled and bewildered Eva at her side.

'Here, Your Honor.' She rose in her seat. 'Gail Brevard, representing Eva Craig.'

The Assistant D.A. also introduced herself.

Judge Cox looked at her over his glasses then glanced down at the copy of the docket in his hand. 'Ms. Brevard? Are you the one filing this motion for OR?'

'Yes, Your Honor. My partner, Conrad

Osterlitz, and I have been retained by Mrs. Craig in this matter, and I would like to resolve the issue of a release on her own recognizance as quickly as possible. My client's health is fragile, and we need to get her in to a more comfortable environment under the care of her private physician.'

'Hmm . . . Ms. Mead? Anything from you on this.'

'Yes, Your Honor.' Ralpha Mead was representing the District Attorney's office. 'We object to the motion for OR on the basis that this is a capital crime and the defendant may well be at risk for flight. If she must be freed for health reasons, we are requesting that a minimum of $500,000 in bail be ordered.'

'That is preposterous, Your Honor!' Gail rose to object. 'Mrs. Craig is well known in the community. She has just suffered a terrible tragedy and is currently under doctor's care. I don't think she's at risk for anything but a complete physical collapse!'

'Counselors, counselors . . . let's try to

come to some sort of reasonable resolution here. I'm inclined to grant release under bail. Let's say, $200,000?' He peered questioningly at Gail.

'Accepted, Your Honor.' Gail knew, from Connie's researches, that Eva had several well-padded funds at her disposal. Obtaining the money for bail would be no problem, and it was in her client's best interest to get her into a better situation. Eva said nothing, for which Gail was grateful.

Mead accepted the arrangement as well, and once the papers had been signed and filed, Eva was free to go. Gail gave Hugo a quick call and he was at their side the moment they left the building. A few local curiosity-seekers were lingering about the parking lot, including the stringer for the News. 'Any comments?' he called out, but Gail shook her head firmly, and Hugo steered the women into his waiting van.

Once Eva had been safely ensconced in her suite at the Lodge, Gail tried once more to reach her client's doctor. She shook her head as she put down the phone. 'He's not taking my calls, Hugo. I'm beginning to think he doesn't want any part of this.'

'Do you want me to go over there, see if I can get some kind of response?'

'No. That's probably not a good idea. Let me talk to Eva again and see if there's anyone else she can call. I don't like the thought of leaving her alone right now.'

★　★　★

Eventually, Eva suggested Gail contact an elderly couple, Marta and Maurice, who'd been long-time employees of the Craigs. They were quite willing to come in and see to Eva's needs while she stayed at the Lodge, and Gail retained them on the spot. Eva still seemed at a loss as to why her doctor hadn't contacted her. 'I can't imagine what the problem is,' she said. 'He's always been very accommodating.'

Gail wondered if the doctor had been listening to the gossip proliferating about the tiny mountain community like wildfire, and had decided he wanted nothing more to do with the Craig family. Eva then suggested they call a homeopathic practitioner, a woman named Ingrid, whose services she had used from time to time, and who agreed to come to the Lodge and see if there was 'anything she could do' for her client.

'Better than nothing,' Gail said to Hugo over coffee. 'At least she won't be by herself.'

A few moments later, Connie pushed through the big double doors into the lobby, sank down gratefully in a lounge chair, and gulped the iced tea they thrust at him. 'That tastes great. The traffic was murder coming up the hill. I got stuck behind a tour bus going about twenty miles an hour. Have you guys eaten yet? I'm starved.'

The three moved over to the restaurant area, where they unanimously ordered the house specialty.

'That hits the spot,' sighed Connie, as he sank his teeth into a tender piece of meat. 'Now, for my news.'

'What did you find?' Gail was curious about the Craig financial empire, and especially about the circumstances concerning Linda's death and Win's subsequent marriage to Eva.

'Well, that's what's so interesting. Apparently all the real money in the household belongs to Eva. Of course, we all know Win made a good living, both as a lawyer and later as a judge. But the really big bucks were brought to the marriage by Eva, not the other way around. I'm still trying to follow the money trail, but she inherited a goodly bit of it, first from her parents, who both passed away in the 1950s, and later from her first husband, who died of what appears to be natural causes, just a year or so before Win's first wife, Linda, passed away.'

'Appears?' Gail wasn't the only one to pick up on the obvious, as Hugo gave a low whistle and shook his head.

'Yeah, well, that's the most interesting part. Eva's first husband was one Otto von Lichtenberg, an *émigré* who showed up here not long after the Second World War with a fortune in artwork and precious gems. She was years younger than he was, and when he died suddenly, from an apparent heart attack, she was his only surviving heir. Any other relatives had died during the war. There was some question about the circumstances surrounding his death, since there'd been a fire in the house . . . '

'A fire?' Gail said.

'Yes. The fire had gone out, but his body was discovered in the bedroom where it had started. The investigators came to the conclusion that he had suffered a heart attack while trying to extinguish the flames.'

'Where was Eva when all this took place?'

'Visiting friends. She had left the house earlier in the evening to keep a prior dinner engagement. He stayed home because he was a bit 'under the weather,' as she had put it. The friends vouched for her, and nothing more came of it. Oh yes, she had him cremated a few days later, so even if there had been anything to discover, the evidence was all neatly discarded.' Connie spread butter over a roll and bit into it hungrily. 'Guess who else was cremated?'

'I'm afraid to ask, but if I had to guess, I'd bet my bottom dollar it was Linda Craig, Win's *first* wife. Am I right?'

'Bingo. And here's something else. A friend and companion had 'volunteered' to care for Linda Craig during her final days. Want to take another wild guess who that 'friend and companion' was?'

'Eva von Lichtenberg?'

'Right again. And the friends she was visiting when dear old Otto came to such a fiery end? Judge and Mrs. Winston Craig, whose winter home in Palm Springs was not far from the von Lichtenberg estate in nearby Palm Desert. I think we have a real problem on our hands here, people. One of the first things we need to do is make absolutely sure that no one, and I mean *no one*, gets to see Eva until we do some more research on her background. I don't trust the lady with the purple gloves, and I think we need to be very careful about our next steps. I understand we have contracted to 'protect and defend' her.

But I also don't want to risk anyone's safety, either. Do you both agree with me on this?'

Both Hugo and Gail nodded assent.

'I'll hire a local security team to monitor Eva's suite. What do you want *me* to do next?' Hugo was contemplating the ice cream in front of him. He added: 'I suppose a look at Eva's parents might be in order?'

'Yes, and I also think we need to find out as much as possible about Linda's death,' Connie said. 'How old was Joan when her mother died, do you remember?' He turned to Gail.

'Mmm . . . let me see. I'll need to talk to Mother again. Maybe she's found something in Dad's scrapbooks. But it seems to me she must have been about eight or nine. I know Louise was still pretty small. I didn't know her as well, because Joan and I were closer in age. But, yeah, I think the girls would have been in grammar school. Why don't I have a chat with them; maybe they'll remember anything of significance.'

'Okay, sounds like a plan. Just try not to spill the beans too much to the Craig daughters, not until we know more.' Connie tackled his ice cream and chocolate with gusto. 'Now, let's try to relax and enjoy this meal, 'saith the condemned man'.'

Truer words were never spoken.

★　★　★

Later that evening, as Gail and Connie reviewed all the materials in front of them, Gail had a sudden notion. 'I'm just wondering if there might be some connection between this case and the earlier 'Purple Glove' murder. What do you think? Is there any information available on Elisabeta Gutman? It was a long time ago, but there might still be some legal files floating around somewhere.'

'Why don't you ask Joan if she has any objection to you going through the Judge's records?' Connie said. 'I don't know if Reynolds has gotten hold of anything yet, but I'd like to see if that

Gutman case made any waves.'

'I'll try to make my visit to Joan seem like a condolence duty,' Gail said. 'I don't want to just buzz in there and start grilling the poor woman. She's just lost her father, after all.'

'Right. I also don't want to tip our hands too quickly on this. Better by far that we determine what we're dealing with. I suspect we're going to earn our fifty thou, in spades!'

★ ★ ★

Gail tossed and turned through most of the night, but forced herself out of bed early the next morning. She needed to get a head start. She let Connie sleep a bit more. He'd been zonked after the drive to 'San Verdoo' the day before, not to mention the horrendous mountain road traffic on the return trip. Once she had the coffee going, she showered and dressed for the day. She thought about how she would present herself to Joan Foster *née* Craig later that afternoon. While she was considering all this, her phone buzzed.

'Gail? It's Mother. I thought you might like to hear what I found in Dad's old papers.'

'Oh great! I was just about to give you a call. I'm going to try and see Joan later today, and there were a few things I wanted to ask you first.'

'Well, I don't know if this will be any help to you,' Alberta said, 'but I found the mention of Win and Eva's wedding. It was only seven months following Linda's death. I didn't remember at first, but now I do. There was quite a lot of talk about it at the time. People thought he should have waited a bit longer, particularly with the girls being so young.'

'Yes,' Gail said, 'I was wondering about that, too. Do you recall how old they were? When Linda died, I mean?'

'I know Joan was in school. I think she was at least nine. Louise, of course, is about two years younger, so I suppose she would have been in first grade or so. I know it was very hard on them. Linda wasn't sick very long. And, of course, having to adjust to a new stepmother right away . . . yes, there was a lot of talk about that.'

'How did Linda die? Seemed to me it was cancer or something like that.'

'Oh no! It certainly wasn't cancer. She was active right up until a few months before her passing. Used to play tennis, I think, when they were still staying in Palm Springs. Funny, Win sold the desert place right after she died. Said he just couldn't stand to go there anymore, they'd been so happy there. No, it seems to me she died of something like food poisoning, or some mysterious infection. I know it was quick.'

'And she was cremated right away? This is important, Mother.'

'Yes, there was some talk about that, too. You know they had a plot in Montecito. A beautiful spot. But Win said Linda had decided against burial. Said she had changed her mind about all that and asked to be cremated instead. I suppose she left instructions . . . '

'Thanks so much for all this, Mother. You have no idea how this helps.' Mother could be a problem at times, but Gail was thankful now that Alberta was so thorough. At least she had saved all her father's files and knew where everything was. 'Is Erle available? I didn't speak to him last time, and I really should say hello to him.'

After she had talked awhile with her brother, listening to his description of some cartoon he'd been watching, and promising him a 'big slurpy' ice cream on her return, she said goodbye to her mother, reminding Alberta to make a copy of the Craig wedding announcement and anything else she'd discovered in Joe Norris's papers. 'Just run it by the office and they can FAX it to us. Oh, did you happen to find anything about that Purple Glove Murder case?'

'No, but I'm still looking. My goodness, I hadn't realized we'd kept so much. There's a ton of articles and miscellaneous papers in there. I haven't gotten through the half of it yet.'

'Well, keep looking. Again, you have no idea the help you've been, Mother. I can't tell you how much I appreciate it.'

There was a moment of silence, then Alberta Norris cleared her voice. 'Gail, you're my daughter, mine and Joe's. I'll do anything in my power to help you, always. I want you to know that. I've just been thinking, going through these papers, how much you mean to me. I know I don't say it as much as I should, but I am so very proud of you, and I know your father would be too.' She broke off then, and Gail sensed she was crying.

'Thank you, Mother. That means more to me than you could possibly know. Take care — and I love you. Talk to you soon.' She hung up quickly before the mood could be broken by either of them. Not for the first time she reflected on how alike they were — one of the reasons they fought from time to time. She resolved to do better. They didn't make many like Alberta Norris — a truly strong woman. And one, Gail realized now, she had patterned herself after.

★ ★ ★

'Come in, Gail. I was just thinking about you.' Joan led the way into a bright great

53

room located in the guest quarters on the other side of the Craig compound. 'I think we need to talk.'

'I didn't feel like I had much of an opportunity to tell you how truly sorry I am about all this, Joan.' Gail took a seat on a big cushy sofa looking out over the wooded area surrounding the lot. 'I think we may have gotten off to a bad start the other day, and I wanted to assure you that certainly wasn't my intention.'

'I'm just concerned that Eva is 'putting one over' on you. She can be extremely self-serving and manipulative. She certainly had Dad wrapped around her little finger.' Joan busied herself at the bar, then brought over a couple of glasses of sherry and a tray of crackers and cheese. 'Here, help yourself. I haven't had much of an appetite since this happened, but I try to remember other people have to eat.' She grinned awkwardly.

'Thanks, this is perfect.' Gail sipped a bit of the sweet wine and took a cracker. 'I suppose if we'd known what we were getting ourselves into we'd've hesitated a bit more. It just seemed as if Eva was at a

54

complete loss and was really just looking for someone to advise her. We had no idea at the outset that she would be arrested . . . ' Gail looked pointedly at Joan, hoping she would volunteer her thoughts.

'I'll be perfectly honest with you, Gail. I don't like Eva. Never have — and I don't suppose I ever will. Don't get me wrong. She's never done anything I can quite put my finger on. I suppose I resented her so much when she just moved in and took over after Mother died.'

'Wasn't she friends with your mother, to begin with, I mean?'

'Friends — or acquaintances — who knows? They knew each other, that's all. When Mother took sick so suddenly — *voilà!* — there was Eva, ready, willing, and able to step in and take her place.'

'But how long was this before Linda died?' Gail realized she was pushing the issue, but Joan didn't seem to mind.

'She was there from day one. I was still pretty young, and, like most children, I didn't really register what was going on until things got serious. All I remember is that suddenly Mother was extremely ill, people were going about whispering in corners and Dad . . . ' Tears filled Joan's eyes but she angrily brushed them away. ' . . . Dad was simply lost. He didn't seem to know what to do. Then Eva moved in. She just showed up one day, bag in hand, and moved right in! I don't think it was a week later and Mother was gone. I barely remember the funeral. And they had her cremated! I know that wasn't what she wanted, but Eva talked Dad into it! He was like a zombie, wandering around the house without a clue. It was easy for Eva to take over. And then, of course, they were married not long afterwards. I've hated her ever since. And now Dad . . . ' The tears began to flow in earnest, and Gail reached out in support.

'But surely your father and Eva were happy together? They seemed to have a good marriage. Or am I missing something?'

'Eva was very controlling, and Dad just went along with it. I think, after Mother died, something in him died, too — he just gave up. You know she made him get rid of the place in Palm Springs, where he and Mother had been so happy. She said she couldn't stand the desert.'

'But isn't that where she and her first husband lived?'

'Oh, so you know about that, eh? Yes, the 'mysterious Count von Lichtenberg'! Well, he came to a bad end, too.' Joan paused and looked at Gail curiously. 'You know about all that, don't you? You've been looking into Eva's past! *You're* suspicious of her, too!'

'Let's just say we're trying to put all of the pieces of the puzzle together.' Gail didn't really want to get off on this tangent with Joan, but ... 'Is there anything else about Eva's background you think Connie and I should know?'

Joan was silent for a moment then seemed to make up her mind. 'I'm going to tell you something — something I've never told another soul, not even Louise — and you must swear to me you'll never mention it — not to anyone.'

Gail hesitated. 'It's difficult for me to make such a promise to you, without knowing what it is you want to tell me. Legally, I mean.'

'Oh, very well, I'll tell you anyway. You can decide whether or not to use it. But I think you'll agree it's the most bizarre thing you've ever heard. Not long after Mother died, but before Eva and Dad were married, he had to make a business trip out of town. He was to be gone for several days and, even though the house was staffed with servants, he was uncomfortable about leaving Louise and me so soon after our loss. Eva assured him that she would look after us, and he reluctantly left us in her care. Everything went smoothly for the first day or so. But on the second or third day, Louise began to get sick.' Joan paused and took another sip of her sherry. 'Eva ordered the servants to stay away from Louise's room, and I was banned as well, on the grounds that I might 'pick up her flu.' Finally, at the end of the third day, the day before Dad was scheduled to return, I snuck into Louise's room to see how she was doing. As I stood in the doorway, I could see Eva mixing something into a cup of hot

58

cocoa. Just as she was about to lift Louise up to take a sip, she happened to look over and see me standing there in the doorway — she dropped the cup then, spilling the cocoa all over the floor. 'It's all right!' she called out to me. 'Everything's going to be all right. Your sister is better now!' I turned and ran out of the room and back to my own. There was just something about that woman that scared me half to death.

'Later that evening, after I was in bed, but still tossing and turning, the door suddenly opened and there, silhouetted against the light from the hallway, was Eva! I was paralyzed with fear as she tiptoed in and stood over me. There was a large package in her hands and she began to unwrap it, all the time saying, 'It's all right now, *Liebchen*. It's all right!' Finally she pulled the last piece of tissue away and there was a doll. A beautiful porcelain doll. Even at my tender age I could tell it was an antique and probably quite valuable. It was dressed all in lavender silk and had white leather shoes.'

'It was dressed in *lavender*?'

'Yes. And this whole issue of the purple glove! That doll's outfit included purple gloves! I really don't know what to make of all this, Gail. That's why I've been so upset . . . and frightened. You don't know what this woman is capable of. You really don't.' Joan stopped and shook her head.

Gail was silent for a moment. 'Joan, do you still have that doll?'

'No. I got rid of it when I got older. Dad, of course, thought it was a beautiful and thoughtful gift. But I knew, or thought I knew, that she was buying my silence with it. Louise got better and we never spoke of the incident again. But in my heart of hearts I always suspected she had begun doping Louise, perhaps in the same way she had doped Mother. Now Dad is dead under these troubling circumstances, and I can't help thinking . . .'

'All right,' Gail said. 'I'll make you at least one promise. We're keeping Eva monitored in her suite at the Lodge, and I'll insist that she stay there under guard until we get this whole mess cleared up. You can rest assured she won't be back here at the compound as long as there are any questions at all about what happened to your father.' Joan murmured her thanks. 'But in return,' Gail added, 'I'd like to have your permission to peruse your father's old files and records. I think there's more to this than we know, and I'd like to try and follow the thread.'

'I trust you, Gail. God knows I need to be able to trust someone. And I have Louise and our families to be concerned about as well. Yes, by all means. I'll make all the arrangements for you and your team to go through Dad's files. I want to get to the bottom of this as much as anyone. And I think you'll do that with honesty and integrity. I understand that you've been put in the position of defending Eva, but if you find anything, anything at all, that gives you doubt about her innocence, you have my permission to bring it all out into the open.'

Gail rose and gave Joan a quick hug. 'Please extend my condolences to Louise as well as the rest of your families. In the meantime, I'll be in touch over the next few days. I appreciate your trust and candor, Joan. I'll try to be worthy of it.'

★ ★ ★

Gail hurried back to the cabin in order to inform Connie about her conversation with Joan. But strangely, he was nowhere to be found! What's more, he had left no messages, which was not in character. She began trying to reach him on his cell phone, but it kept reverting to voice mail. He wasn't answering. After a few more tries, Gail called Hugo, who did pick up immediately.

'I think we have a problem,' she began.

'Gail! I was just about to call you. Connie's had an accident. I'm with him over at the hospital. You need to get over here right away . . . or do you want me to come get you?'

'Oh my God! Is he all right?' Gail felt her heart drop down to the tips of her toes. Strangely, her first thought was of the vision of Eva, rocking back and forth on the couch that first day, moaning over and over, 'What am I going to do?' Gail was dry-eyed, but felt suddenly as if she had been crying for days.

'He's alive. Just get over here, but for God's sake, drive carefully!'

Twenty minutes later she pulled into the parking lot at the Mountain Hospital. Hugo was watching for her from the steps and ran out to greet her. 'Come on. I'll take you in.'

'What happened, Hugo?'

'He went off the road. I had a look at the car and, Gail . . . it looks to me as if the brakes have been tampered with!'

'You've got to be kidding? What's going on, Hugo? What in God's name have we gotten ourselves into?' Gail was half running now across the parking lot, holding on to Hugo's arm. They reached the entrance and hurried down the hall through the Emergency Ward to a curtained alcove. There they were halted by a uniformed guard.

'Next of kin,' croaked Hugo. 'This is his next of kin.'

'Let me check with the doctor first.' The guard took their names and motioned them back, then stepped inside the curtained area. They heard a few mumbled exchanges, then a gowned physician stepped out. 'Ms. Brevard?'

'Yes. How is he? Can I see him? Can he talk?'

'Whoa! He's had a bad concussion. He's one very lucky guy. He should be all right, but we're running a few tests right now, and I really need you to wait out here until we're through.'

Gail crumpled back into Hugo's arms, and he led her to the waiting area nearby. 'Can I get you anything? Coffee?'

'No. I just can't believe this. Who could have done such a thing?'

'Well, it couldn't have been Mrs. Craig. That was the first thing I checked, and the security team I hired is still in place. She hasn't poked her nose out of the lodge since we deposited her there yesterday.'

'Are you sure it was foul play? Maybe the car slipped on an icy patch.'

'Nope, you know Connie. He's caution personified. I'd bet the farm somebody cut the brake line.'

Gail was silent. The image that came unbidden was that of a woman, standing in the doorway, outlined by light, holding out a package . . . a gift . . . a bribe. Had Eva hoped to purchase their silence with that fifty grand? And was she now trying to assure that silence?

★   ★   ★

'Charles? Gail, here. I've got bad news.' There was a squawking sound from the other end of the line. She gave him the details of Connie's accident. 'Do you think you could put things on hold there awhile and come out? I hate to ask, but we're really in a bind here. We've bitten off just a little more . . . you can? Oh thank you, you don't know how much . . . all right. I'll rent a car for you at Ontario. Can you find your way up . . . or do you want Hugo to meet you? You can? Okay, I'll see you sometime tomorrow.' Gail looked across the table at Hugo and nodded her head. 'He'll be on the first flight out. Should be here by tomorrow afternoon at the latest.'

But true to his word, Charles got the very first standby available to him, and by the time Gail and Hugo broke away from their vigil at the hospital to get a quick bite to eat, Charles was waiting for them back at The Pine Cone. Over a meal, and lots of hot, black coffee, the three operatives plotted their next course of action.

'Hugo, I think we need to start getting down and dirty.' Gail filled them both in on all that Joan had told her, including the bizarre tale about the doll. She felt no compunction about repeating the so-called secret Joan had shared with her. She trusted both Charles and Hugo, and with Connie lying desperately ill in the hospital, it was up to them now to solve this mystery — once and for all. It was obvious to her that the poison in this family had been allowed to fester for too many years. There was something evil and sick going on in the Craig household, and she, for one, was determined to flush it out.

'We need more information on Eva's background, as well as the details of the first Purple Glove Murder.'

She turned to Charles hopefully. 'Do you think you can call in some favors — people you know in Justice — and get into the files on Elisabeta Gutman? What happened to her? Was she ever released from Tehachapi — or did she die there? I assume she would be, at the very least, in her eighties or nineties by now, depending on how old she was when the murder occurred. I'd also be curious about where she and her husband originated. Sounds German or Austrian to me. That would mean some sort of participation in or repercussions from World War II. I'd like to know when they came to this country, what they did for a living. You know the drill. Any other suggestions, Hugo?' she added, turning to the lanky P.I. who was busily jotting down notes of their conversation.

'I can take on looking into the Gutmans' background. I've also had an idea about Jane Brown — you know, the consignment lady — ' he added when both Gail and Charles looked blank. 'There should be some sort of sales and use tax permit info on file in Sacramento. I can also check the Verdugo County Hall of Records to see if there's any kind of FBN (Fictitious Business Name) listed for her there. If she had anything at all to do with concealing that glove, she might know more.'

Charles wiped his mouth and pushed aside his plate. 'Sounds like a plan. I'll start dredging through my Justice contacts and see if I can find any records on the Gutman woman. What about Judge Craig's files?'

'I thought I'd tackle those myself. I need to get back over to the hospital and check on Connie first. They have all our cell phone numbers in case we need to be notified of any change in his condition but, honestly . . . ' Gail paused and shook her head. Charles reached over and patted her encouragingly. ' . . . Honestly, I think we can accomplish more by staying busy and trying to solve this damnable situation, than sitting around the hospital waiting for the news. Now, let's get going. And please, call me from time to time, just

68

to let me know you're both all right, and to keep me up on what you've discovered.'

'Lock and load!' Hugo scraped his chair back, grabbed the check before either of them could move, and headed for the check-out counter.

'All right.' Charles helped Gail with her jacket. 'Let's go get 'em!'

★   ★   ★

'He's holding his own,' Doctor McDonnell confirmed. He was middle-aged, prematurely gray and seemed to Gail to be concerned and compassionate about his patients — she was thankful Connie had landed in such good care. 'He came through the operation all right. We got the hemorrhage sutured and it appears to be holding. All we can do is to wait and see how he does over the next twenty-four hours or so. He's resting comfortably, so it's probably better not to disturb him right now . . . '

'Of course,' Gail said. Everything in her wanted to go to Connie's side and cheer him on, but he seemed to be stable, and, from all appearances, in very good hands. 'Thank you so much for everything you've done and are doing. I have things I need to do, but please call me if there is any change at all, or if you think I need to get back here. You have my associates' numbers as well. If for some reason you can't reach me, please call one of them.'

'I will,' the doctor said. 'You go do what you need to do. We'll take care of Mr. Osterlitz. We'll call you immediately if you need to return.'

Gail hurried out to the parking lot, collected her car, and set out for the Craig compound. Joan was waiting for her as she drove in and parked near the door. 'How's Connie? Oh my God, we had no idea, did we, how terrible this was all going to get — as if it wasn't bad enough.' Tears came to her eyes as she quickly embraced Gail and pulled her in to the warmth and shelter of the house. Turning right, as Eva had done a few days earlier, she led the way into the Judge's inner sanctum. A fire was crackling in the fireplace and a coffee urn and plate of sandwiches sat nearby. 'I didn't know if you'd eaten yet,' Joan gestured at the folding table covered in a starchy white cloth, 'but I just wanted you to be comfortable while you work. All of Dad's files, all we could find anyway, from the beginnings of his legal practice until he was elected Justice of the Peace, are in those.' She indicated a series of vintage oak file cabinets in one corner. 'I know it doesn't look like much, but you have to remember that some of them may have been purged from time to time. I just hope enough remains for you to find the information you need. Now, I know you want to get started, so I'll leave you alone and see that you're not disturbed.' She gave Gail a quick peck on the cheek then left the room, shutting the door firmly behind her.

Gail poured a cup of coffee, then glanced about the room to get her bearings. She had an idea of the dates involved for the Gutman case, and her only hope was that the Judge's files were in as good an order as Joe Norris's. She quickly folded up the white tablecloth

71

and laid it to one side. She needed a solid flat surface to work. She sat down the coffee cup, placed her cell phone face up next to it, opened her briefcase, and pulled out her sheaf of notes. Dates . . . she needed some idea of dates.

If she went back sixty years, which would take it back to around 1950 . . . but World War II had ended in 1945, and displaced persons and refugees had begun immigrating shortly thereafter. It would have taken Elisabeta Gutman and her husband at least a year or so to get established, she thought, so perhaps 1946 would be a good place to start. She knew that Judge Craig had left private practice by the 1970s, so probably she was looking at no more than a twenty-year window at the most. That much decided, she moved over to the filing cabinet in the furthest corner and opened the top drawer. Quickly scanning through several files and the dates on the earliest pages, she saw that these files were mostly from the early 1940s, in the midst of World War II, and earlier than her search scope. She picked a drawer in the middle of the cabinet and found the first paper in the first file was dated January 10, 1945. The War in Europe was not quite over. She moved to the bottom drawer and couldn't believe her eyes. The very first file was dated January 1, 1946! Here is where she'd start. She began pulling out files from the drawers and carrying them over to her worktable, stack by stack. She planned to go through each file, one by one, until she found something (anything she hoped!) having to do with the Gutmans or the trial

She quickly grew discouraged. Most of the cases were civil suits, with the occasional divorce, estate, and probation and the like. It was eating up a lot of time, leafing through all these files, and then carrying them back to the filing cabinet to return with another load. She thought about it a minute, then pulled her chair over to the cabinets. She was through now with the first cabinet, and had moved to the second drawer of the second cabinet. She quickly glanced at the first page in the first file. April 15, 1949. The page indicated this was an estate settlement. She glanced through and saw nothing of interest. Still, this process was much quicker. Systematically, she continued through each and every file in all the drawers of the second cabinet. Nothing!

She went back, filled her half-empty cup, and sat down at the fireplace for a moment to rest. Glancing at her watch, she realized that several hours had passed and sighed. How in God's name would she ever get through all this? She might have to call Hugo and Charles in to help at some point. She could only hope they were having better luck than she was.

As if in answer to her prayer, her cell phone buzzed. She jumped up and grabbed it. 'Gail Brevard,' she said. An icy nugget of fear dropped into her heart. What if Connie . . . ?

'Hi, babe.' It was Hugo. 'Through the records in Sacramento I've turned up the real name of Jane Brown. It's Janette Braun, not Brown. My guess is that it was just an easier spelling. You know, it's not uncommon for people to simplify their names for business reasons.'

'Yeah, I guess you're right. Well, keep digging. See if you can find her. I'm curious how she got hold of Eva's consignment items. Have you heard from Charles?'

'Nope, not a peep. No news . . . I guess. How're you doing?'

'Nothing yet. You guys may have to come help me with this at some point. There's a lot of stuff to go through. I'm not ready to throw in the towel yet, though. Keep digging. Thanks for everything.'

'You're welcome. If I haven't found any more in another hour or so, I'll swing by and see if I can give you a hand. Want me to call Charles?'

'No, let him be. He knows what he's doing. Let's just hope he finds out more than we have so far! Keep in touch.'

Gail shook the cobwebs out of her brain and went over to the window. Like the nearby sitting room, the office boasted a spectacular view overlooking the lake. Gail could imagine the Judge sitting here, enjoying the sight, as he worked on his files, papers, memoirs, perhaps . . . Memoirs! She raced back to the table, stuffed her cell phone into a pocket, and ran out the door. Collaring a maid, she asked her to find Joan as quickly as possible.

Joan came rushing back into the office, breathless from some outdoor activity she had been supervising with the children. 'What is it? Did you find something?'

'No. Sorry, I didn't mean to get your hopes up, but I just wanted to ask if your father had ever written any memoirs. You know, anything about his life and work. I got to thinking about it, and I thought he might have mentioned some of his more interesting or important cases. Just a shot in the dark . . . '

'Of course, I don't know why I didn't think of it. Since his retirement he's been working on the family genealogy, and in conjunction with that, I think he was also penning an autobiographical account as well. I'd completely forgotten about it until you mentioned the possibility just now. And I know where it is, too. He was working toward getting it all compiled to his satisfaction. Then he was going to publish it privately for the family members. Hand it out at Christmas probably. He didn't want anyone to see it until then, though. Said he wanted it to be a surprise for the kids. Here.' She turned to an armoire on the other side of the room. She opened it to reveal neatly stacked boxes containing manuscript sheets. There were perhaps a dozen of them.

'Now, I think he had these organized by family. You know, his father's family, his mother's family, and so forth. But then there were a couple of boxes that contained his autobiography. I honestly don't know how far he got with it. We weren't supposed to look at them. I guess I should try and complete this now. Make sure the children get copies . . . ' Joan fell into a nearby chair and dissolved into tears.

'We'll help you with that.' Gail said. 'Now, with your permission, I'll see if I can find what I need in the biographical material. Please, go on back to the kids and let me take care of things here. We'll get this sorted out, I promise.'

Snuffling, Joan nodded and left the

room. Gail surveyed the boxes, then selected what seemed to be the most likely pair, setting to one side of what were obviously the genealogical records. She carefully carried the boxes over to the table and seated herself, said a little prayer, and opened the first one. Only time would tell if their answers lay here.

★ ★ ★

Gail sat back in the easy chair near the fire and stretched. She had finally moved over here to read through the story of Winston Craig's life. She had a pad at her side, and from time to time, she jotted down notes. She skimmed over the early years, the anecdotes about his parents, childhood memories, school years, and the like, until finally she got to the part about his work. He had begun practicing law on his own just before the close of World War II, and had quickly made a name for himself as a brilliant and capable litigator. He had continued building the business, adding to his reputation over the next twenty years or so, when friends convinced him to run for Justice of the Peace in Verdugo County. The local Congressman supported his bid, and he won handily over an unpopular older incumbent. He was re-elected two more times, then retired for good, following the sudden death of his first wife, Linda. With two small daughters to raise, it was understandable he would remarry, and his choice of his wife's friend and companion during her final illness, Eva von Lichtenberg, did not raise too many eyebrows.

So far, all this was pretty much what they already knew. But Gail kept reading and, toward the end of the account, she was overjoyed to see that the Judge indeed had gone back to reprise some of his more interesting cases. As she skimmed the dates and names, she suddenly stopped, marked the spot with her finger, and turned to gaze out over the lake. She thought awhile then, very carefully, began putting the Judge's manuscript back in its box. One page, and one page only, did she withhold and place in her briefcase. Punching a few numbers into her phone, she spoke quickly into the receiver. She listened a moment, nodded to herself, then broke the connection.

'Did you find anything?' Joan asked anxiously as Gail said goodbye.

'I'm not sure yet, but I'll let you know the moment we have anything concrete. For now, just try and relax as much as you can. I'll get back to you as quickly as possible.'

'Take care, Gail. Please take care,' Joan said, then closed the door.

* * *

In the meantime, Charles Walton had been working the phones nonstop, querying anyone he could think of who might have some idea where criminal court records from the 1950s and '60s would be filed, and just how accessible they might be. He finally got a lead from an old court clerk he'd dealt with frequently in his early years as an L.A. County Prosecutor.

'Yep, I think they're prob'ly in the

vault. Som'thin' that old, fer sure. If they haven't been 'stroyed altogether, that is . . .'

'Thanks Hiram. If there's a payday on this one, I'll buy you a cuppa, OK?' Charles was known around the old Halls of Justice for his generosity, and the 'cuppa' would more than likely work into a nice tip for Hiram.

'Thanks, Boss. Take care now. Hope you finds what yer lookin' fer.'

Charles shuddered at the thought of traipsing through the vault, a notoriously cold and drafty storage area beneath the old County Court House, full of cobwebs and rat litter. Still, if he could find the missing files, it would help his friends, Gail and Connie. They'd given him the opportunity of his lifetime, setting him up in the Tucson office, and he owed them everything. He gulped a moment, thinking of Connie lying near death in the hospital. Anything — he'd do anything at all for them, come what may.

★ ★ ★

'Aha!' Hugo muttered to himself. He had just completed a frustrating session of accessing one of the stand-up computers open to the public in the waiting room at the Verdugo County Hall of Records. After fiddling with the online database for twenty minutes or so, he finally figured out how to work his way into the information he needed on DBAs and FBNs. He tried several combinations of words and names — and there it was — the name he was looking for.

'Hmm. Let's see what Gail can do with *this*,' he said, jotting down a few notes and running off some copies. 'Now, on to Probate . . . '

Just as he got back out to the van, his phone chimed. Checking to be sure he hadn't mislaid anything, he settled back in the seat and hit 'Talk.'

'Hugo? Gail, here. I think we can start wrapping this up. I just talked to Charles and he's getting on the freeway now to head out. It may take him an hour or two, depending on traffic. Where are you?'

'I'm just leaving the Hall of Records. I've got some interesting stuff. I'll be heading up the hill as soon as I gas up. Is there anything else you need me to do down here? If not, I'll get going.'

'No. I think we've got everything we need. By the way, I just talked to Dr. McDonnell. Connie's recovered consciousness. They think he's out of danger, so that's another plus. Now, here's what I want you to do, once you get back . . . ' She proceeded to outline what she needed.

'All right, that's it. I'll see you soon.'

* * *

She had one last call to make. 'Detective Reynolds? Gail Brevard. I have a favor to ask. My team and I have uncovered some information which I think will be relevant, both to the investigation into Judge Craig's death, and also to my partner's so-called automobile 'accident'.'

'How is Mr. Osterlitz? Yes, I heard about all that and I wanted to tell you how sorry we are about his injury. I'll be glad to assist in any way I can, officially, of course.'

'Of course. I'd like to ask you to join us this evening at my cabin. I think you'll be very interested in what we have to show you. Then, with your permission, we may be able to conclude both of our investigations on a satisfactory note.'

'I'll be there. And I'm looking forward to seeing what you've put together. Shall we say around six? Fine.'

* * *

The next morning, after a quick light breakfast, Gail prepared for what she hoped would be the final steps in the solution to the Craig case. She dressed carefully, in a light gray flannel pants suit, a green silk blouse, and emerald and diamond studs in her ears. It was important that she looked not only professional, but non-threatening. Everything depended on her innate talent and ability to draw out witnesses, and this occasion would be no different than what might take place in a standard court trial. She double-checked the contents of her briefcase, and the small box of other records and materials she was bringing as back up. Hugo and Charles, who were bunking together in the Lodge suite, were already setting the scene. Detective Reynolds would also be hovering in the background, she supposed. She had asked him to stay available but concealed, so as not to scare away their prey. Hugo had set up microphones in the room so that Reynolds would be able to hear every-thing that was said — and to intervene at once, if necessary.

She had finally been able to speak to Connie. He was groggy, but seemed alert and in good spirits. She had given him a brief rundown of their efforts, but spared him all the details. Better not to let too much of this get out until they were sure.

As she made the brief drive to the Lodge, she glanced out at the lake once more. This morning seemed different somehow. The water was a deeper blue, the light from the pale sun more filtered. A change of season was in the air. Suddenly she yearned for home. Her own comfortable space called to her. The vacation here had been great, right up until Craig's death. But now she was tired of it all, and wanted nothing more than to get back to her normal routine. As soon as Connie was able to travel again, they could all head back: Charles to Tucson, and she, Connie, and Hugo to Cathcart. She needed a long hot soak in her own tub to clear all the muck from her body and soul. And she and Erle needed to make a deposit.

* * *

'I've asked you to join me here,' Gail began, thinking through her words carefully, 'because, as you know, Mr. Osterlitz was injured badly in the accident. He's been in a coma for the last few days, and it's been extremely difficult for me to function properly.'

'Oh yes! We've all been so sorry about all that,' Eva broke in. She was dressed in a pale lavender chiffon number. What looked to be genuine pearls hung in a triple cluster around her neck, and two large natural pearls swung in pendants from her earlobes. 'Will he be all right, do you think?'

'The doctors are optimistic for a complete recovery, but, of course, anything might still go wrong.' Gail paused. Her next words would be critical.

'Mr. and Mrs. Goodman,' she said, turning to the elderly couple. Maurice and Marta, sitting uncomfortably on straight chairs near the door, straightened up.

'Yes, ma'am?' Marta rose immediately. 'Is there anything . . . ?'

'Oh no, Marta, nothing right at the moment. I was just going to ask if there was any reason you both couldn't stay on with Mrs. Craig indefinitely. I mean, do you have any ties or other responsibilities you need to attend to?'

'No, ma'am.' Marta glanced at her husband. 'No, I think that would be very satisfactory. We have no other job right now. We'd be glad of the chance to be of service to Eva — er, Mrs. Craig, I mean.'

'That's all right. I suppose you've known Eva for a good many years, haven't you?'

Marta looked a little uncomfortable. 'Well, we were with the family for many years . . . '

'The *Craig* family, was that? Or was it the von Lichtenbergs?'

Maurice broke in. 'Oh no, it was the Craigs, wasn't it, *Liebchen*?'

'That's interesting, because you seem to be of German — or is it Austrian — background? And 'von Lichtenberg,' of course . . . well, you can see how I might be confused.' Gail smiled reassuringly at the couple. 'And 'Goodman?' Was that your original name? When you were still in Europe, I mean?'

Maurice stood up. 'I think we will go now. You have other things to do, I suppose. We must prepare the lunch . . . '

'Oh, we're having lunch served here by the Lodge. I think you should stay.' Maurice sat down again, but gave Marta a meaningful look.

'Now, the other person I wanted to talk to today was you, Ingrid.' The self-styled homeopathic healer had been sitting silently on the other side of the room, taking in the conversation with the

Goodmans. 'I was wondering if you, too, might be interested in a full-time position as a companion of sorts to Mrs. Craig. She'll be alone now, I suppose, in that great big beautiful house. I'm sure she would be happy to have someone compatible there with her.' Gail glanced at Eva, who was looking at her in consternation. 'Would you be available for such a job?'

'No! No!' Ingrid suddenly jumped to her feet. 'No, I can't do this! Please, I must leave now!' She made for the door, but just as she reached it, it opened and Detective Reynolds, accompanied by two of his uniformed officers, stepped through.

'Now, Ms. Brown, or should I say, 'Braun.' I don't think you're going anywhere, not just yet.'

'My name isn't Braun! It's Goodman! Ingrid Goodman! *Tell them*!' she screamed at Maurice and Marta. 'Tell them!'

Hugo stepped forward then. 'Are you the 'Ingrid Goodman' who is listed with the Verdugo County Hall of Records with a Fictitious Business Name of 'Janette

Brown'? And, under the DBA 'Janette Brown,' do you have a Sales and Use Permit on file in Sacramento for the State of California? And, are you also the 'Jane Brown' who leases Consignment Booth #230 at the Things Remembered Antique Store in Glen Falls, where you sell used and vintage clothing?'

Ingrid crumpled back on her seat with a moan. 'Papa, Mama — what shall I say?'

Marta moved to her side and cradled her in her arms. 'It's all right, *Liebchen*. We'll be all right. We always are.'

Gail looked over at Charles. It was his turn now. He rose, and with a true litigator's stance, cleared his throat and began: 'Maurice Goodman — or should I say, *Gutman*? — are you, as various court records on file in Los Angeles County indicate, the younger brother of one Michael Gutman, who died, or was killed, in a fire which was proven to have been set on September 30, 1959 at the premises near here owned by him and his then wife, Elisabeta Gutman? And was Elisabeta Gutman tried and convicted of the premeditated murder of Michael Gutman, then sentenced to life in the Women's Prison at Tehachapi, where she died of uterine cancer on August 4, 1969? And, because of the nature of her conviction, were all the worldly assets of both Michael and Elisabeta Gutman, which included not only the mountain property, but money, jewelry, and artwork they had brought to this country from Europe following World War II, were not all those assets conveyed by probate to their only child, a daughter ... ' He turned slightly. ' ... a daughter by the name of Evalina Gutman?'

There was an audible gasp in the room from Joan and Louise Craig, who had been sitting quietly to one side, taking all this in with great curiosity.

'No! No! Please don't do this!' Eva looked wildly to one side then another, seeking for sympathy where none lay. 'I can explain!' she added. 'Please, let me explain ... '

'I'm sure we'll all be happy for that,' Gail said. 'But first things first. Didn't you use 'Braun' as your maiden name, when you were first married by arrangement of your two families to Otto von Lichtenberg? Why did you use the name 'Braun'? And what is its significance?'

'Braun was *my* maiden name,' broke in Marta. 'When there was all the unpleasantness over Michael's death, the decision was made,' she glanced at Maurice. 'We made the decision to change the names of both girls — ' Here she indicated the cousins, Eva and Ingrid. 'We chose to give them my name so that they wouldn't have to carry that terrible burden any longer.'

'And following Linda Craig's death,' Gail said, 'when Eva convinced Winston to marry her, he discovered her true identity in the records. Didn't he try to convince you to admit to it, Eva? You see, in the genealogical records he was compiling, he had already changed your name back to 'Gutman'.'

'Had he? I didn't know that . . . ' Eva seemed puzzled and looked searchingly at the Goodmans and her cousin, Ingrid. 'I think there was a lot that went on I didn't know.'

'Well, he seemed particularly intrigued about the connection between you two, and the fact that he had tried to save your mother from being convicted of killing your father. That must have been difficult for him. Resolving that issue in his mind, I mean.' Gail hesitated. 'But, I guess the most important question I have now is this: how long have your aunt and uncle, Maurice and Marta, and your cousin, Ingrid, been living under your patronage, Eva? How long?'

'Always. It was my responsibility to care for all of them. The money, my parents' money, it was family money, you see. It wasn't just mine. My father was the eldest son, so he inherited. But when he died, and when my mother . . . ' Her face crumpled like old paper. ' . . . When my mother went to prison, it was me who inherited. The law would have it no other way. But I couldn't do that, could I? Just leave them out in the cold — with nothing. So I contrived a way for them always to be cared for. To always be under my wing of protection. Yes, we changed our names. It's done all the time. There was no attempt to defraud anyone.

'But there was always bitterness. Yes,' she shook her head at her relatives, 'yes, I know there was. None of you ever quite forgave me for it. So, things began to happen. First there was Otto. No, it wasn't a marriage for love. But our families had arranged it from my birth, and once I was grown, Maurice insisted on contacting him again and holding him to the agreement. And Otto was kind to me. It was he, *Liebchen* . . . ,' she turned to Joan. 'He gave me the doll I gave you. He always thought I was more like a little girl than a real woman. So he thought I would like the doll. But then he died. Terribly. Suddenly. How frightened he must have been.' She glanced sideways at Maurice. '*You* did that, didn't you? I was sure of it from the beginning. The way you acted. Then, of course, there was Linda. Once Otto was out of the way, there had to be a new conquest. And Judge Craig, Winston, was their next choice for me. Marta inserted herself into the Craig household. Then suddenly my friend Linda was sick and near death. Maurice pushed me, once more, to go to Judge Craig and offer my services. I couldn't refuse. Maurice had a hypnotic power over me, and threatened to expose my background to everyone. I couldn't allow that. So I did it. And then she died. And Win and I were married.

'Then, there were those terrible three days when Louise took ill.' She glanced over at the two Craig girls, huddled together in horror. 'It took all my homeopathic skills to come up with the antidote. And I kept giving it to her until, finally, blessedly, she recovered. That was when I brought you the doll, Joan. It was like a promise to you. A promise that I would never allow anything to happen to you girls.

'And now there is Win . . . ' She hung her head and sobbed. 'I couldn't stop it. Couldn't keep it from happening. I think now that one of them, Marta or Maurice, must have seen his entries in the family genealogy. They always felt so threatened, were so ashamed by what had happened. They could not allow him to go forward with that book. One of them must have taken my pills and the gloves, and set that horrible sequence in motion.'

'And Connie,' Gail interrupted. 'What about the brake lines on the car? Did you think he was getting to close to the truth? Were you going to kill all of us?' She turned in fury to the Goodmans.

'We had nothing to do with that.' Maurice said. He stared stonily ahead. 'I don't know how that happened.'

'Well, I think I can shed a little light on that,' drawled Hugo. 'When Connie first became uncomfortable about Mrs. Craig here, right after she was released on OR, he had me set up a security perimeter around her suite. He was mostly concerned about *her*, you see, so we kept a tight watch on her. She never left the suite during that whole period of time. So, in my opinion, she didn't have the opportunity, nor . . . ' He gazed appraisingly at the frail woman. ' . . . Nor did she have the physical strength required to sabotage Connie's car. On the other hand . . . ' He swung around toward Ingrid. 'Ms. Brown or Goodman here, as she prefers to be known. She was clocked leaving Mrs. Craig's suite just a few hours before the accident. She had plenty of time to get down there and cut those lines. What's more . . . ' He squinted at the fit, well-muscled woman. ' . . . She looks to me like she'd be physically capable of it, as well.' He sat back down.

Ingrid, who had moved over beside her parents during the interrogations, suddenly made a break for the door. Detective Reynolds stepped aside and let her dash through — into the arms of the waiting officers outside.

'Ingrid Goodman, also known as Jane or Janette Brown: You are under arrest for tampering with an automobile belonging to one Conrad Osterlitz with the intent of doing great bodily harm.' He turned abruptly to Maurice and Marta. 'Maurice and Marta Braun Gutman or Goodman, as you are known: you are both under arrest for the murders of Otto von Lichtenberg, Linda Craig, and Winston Craig.' He read everyone their rights, then his officers took the three off to the Justice

Court and the holding quarters there.

'Of course, we'll need to examine thoroughly all the evidence you've presented today, as well as make further investigations of our own,' he said to Gail as they wrapped things up. 'But I have to say, I think we finally have the truth of the matter, as much as we'll ever know. Great job, Counselor. I'll be sorry to see you all leave the area.'

'I can't say we'll be sorry to go,' she said, glancing at Hugo and Charles, who nodded their agreement. 'Still, we may be back — the next time we crave excitement! Nothing like a little murder in the pines to keep the adrenaline flowing! How about it, guys — how about some rib-eyes before we go tell Connie how we solved the Purple Glove Murder case!'

A DEATH AT CLIFFSIDE

Gail paused a moment while sipping from her Chardonnay to gaze at the lovely scene before them. 'Whoops! There it goes!' she said, gesturing toward the huge orange ball of a sun settling into the Bay. 'God, what a view! Thanks so much, Nick, for suggesting this place. I'd heard of it, but had no idea what a treat it'd be.'

Gail Brevard and her law partner and companion, Conrad Osterlitz, were enjoying a working vacation in San Francisco. They and their associate, Charles Walton, had made the trip to meet with Charles's cousin, Nick Quintaine, the nephew and only surviving heir of Floyd Seymour, a real estate investor and entrepreneur back in Gail's hometown of Cathcart.

On this particular evening the four were enjoying a high-end dinner at the Julius's Castle, a scenic restaurant overlooking the City by the Bay at the top of the fabled brick Lombard Street, which zigzags back and forth down Telegraph Hill.

'The food can be so-so,' Nick said, twirling the wine in his glass, 'but the view is worth every penny.'

Gail could have read innuendo into that comment, if she'd cared to, but with Connie at her side, she chose to let it slide. She and Nick had been an item, briefly, not so long ago; but things had gone wrong between them during the Powell trial, and they'd parted company, with their friendship miraculously intact.

'How are Floyd and Nancy doing?' Gail referred to the Seymours, who'd been on the other side of Damon Powell's murder trial, and subsequently, the cause of the break-up between Nick and Gail.

'Uncle Floyd's doing fine. He's bounced back from everything pretty well. I've been a little more concerned about Aunt Nancy. It seems to me that she just sort of gave up after — well, everything.' He shrugged and turned to Charles Walton, his cousin by marriage, and the fourth member of their party. 'What do you think, Chuck?'

'Oh, I don't know.' Charles hated the

family nickname and had to bite his tongue whenever it was used, which was frequently when he was around Nick. They all still seemed to see him as the chubby-cheeked little 'Chuckie,' instead of the serious litigator and head of Connie's Tucson office. He counted to ten and tackled the antipasto platter in the center of the table with gusto. 'I think she'll be all right — eventually. She has plenty to do, now that she's gotten more involved in the business.'

'Well, I hope that's true,' Gail said. She skipped a beat, amused. She knew how Charles felt about his nickname. 'And how *is* their business doing, Nick? I've heard mixed opinions from Mother.'

'I think they'll weather the storm, as usual. It looks to me like the high-end real estate market is getting ready to rebound in Cathcart. You know, there'll always be people with money looking for another overpriced mansion to buy.' Nick chuckled. 'I wouldn't be surprised if they didn't end up back on top of the heap again. At least that's what I'm hoping. Speaking of which — '

And the conversation drifted back to their reason for being there in the first place, the upkeep and future of the Seymour Mall. 'Some of the shops really need a facelift,' Gail said. She'd hoped to obtain Nick's permission for some extended renovations in the sprawling shopping center at the heart of Cathcart's business district. 'I think you'd see a big return for your money there. Why don't you try to get Nancy interested in updating some of those little shops and boutiques? It might be a good role for her, as well as therapeutic. I know she has a real designer's touch.'

'Let me talk to them about it. I'm inclined to agree with you — about the upgrades, I mean. But I've got to convince Uncle Floyd it would be money well-spent. If I can get Nancy to come on board, I imagine it won't be difficult to get him interested in the project as well.' Nick paused to butter a roll.

'In the meantime,' he said, 'I've got another matter to discuss with you. I've gone back and forth about whether even to bring it up or not. I think I'm too close to the whole thing to evaluate it properly, so I'd really appreciate your opinion.'

Gail glanced at Connie. He raised an eyebrow, his signal for: 'Let's see what this is all about.'

'Well, don't leave us hanging, Nick,' she said, helping herself to one of the crab cakes. 'What's the mystery?'

Nick glanced out at the cityscape beneath them. Purple shadows were gathering and colorful lights were twinkling everywhere. Before long the backdrop would be like black velvet, intersected with brilliant streaks outlining the many busy streets crisscrossing down to the Bay.

'A friend of mine has died,' he began, 'under mysterious circumstances — '

A hush seemed to hover over their table. A waiter was coming around to light the candles and check on their drinks. They waited until he had completed his tasks, then Connie broke the silence: 'Tell us about it. We'd like to help, if we can.'

Nick cleared his throat. 'Well, first I should give you a little background. As you're aware, I've lived in the Bay Area for most of my adult life. After attending the University of California Berkeley for my graduate degree, I worked for a local architect named Bobby Burrell. It wasn't a coincidence that one of my old classmates was his daughter, Cele.' He paused as the waiter began serving their meal. 'Cele eventually landed a job on a local rag in Novato as a society stringer. She'd been working there for a few years when she heard of an opening on the *World-News*.' Nick was referring to the premier Sacramento newspaper. 'She applied for and was hired as their restaurant critic. At the same time, her father was looking for an associate with experience in structural engineering, my major. I jumped at the opportunity to work with him, since he had a great reputation in the field.' He took an appreciative bite of the tasty veal *osso buco* in front of him.

'What happened?' Gail interposed. She knew that, at some point, Nick had gone into business for himself. Of course, these days, most of Nick's time was occupied with assisting his uncle with the family's enterprises, but she knew he still had an affinity for building things, and had helped maintain the business entity of the structural engineering firm he'd founded.

'To make a long story short,' Nick continued, 'Burrell suffered a fatal heart attack not long after I'd joined the team. His son, Bobby, Jr., took over, and it soon became clear that we had differences in philosophy about the direction of the business. I checked out, cashed in the stock options I'd accumulated, and with Uncle Floyd's blessings and support, opened my own firm. It was smaller, but I was my own boss, and I was certainly less stressed. At the same time, Cele and I, while remaining friends over the years, had begun to drift apart as well. I honestly hadn't given much thought to any of the Burrells until I read in the *World-News* . . . .' He smiled wryly. ' . . . That she'd married a Pulitzer Prize-winning reporter by the name of Timmy Lerner. You've heard of him, I'm sure. He was the one who spent a year undercover as 'Tomás Príncipe' to break the El Gato Gordo Scandal in the State

Capitol, which resulted in the conviction and imprisonment of Governor Alberto Correa.' Connie nodded — the story had even made CNN. 'I was happy for her, of course, and hoped she'd have a good life.'

'But . . . ?' Connie echoed out loud the question in each of their minds. ' . . . Something went wrong?' He wiped his mouth on the huge snowy white cloth napkin, and pushed back the plate containing what was left of his juicy prime rib.

'Yes, something went very wrong.' The waiter came around again to refresh their wine glasses and take their orders for dessert. Nick waited until they were alone once more, then continued. 'Several months ago I heard through the grapevine from a mutual friend that Cele had given birth to a baby boy. I didn't think too much about it at the time, beyond wondering if I should try to send a gift. She hadn't really kept in touch with me after her marriage, but I hated for it to end on a sour note. I didn't want her to think I was bitter about our break-up — or her marriage.'

This conversation was hitting a little too close to home for Gail's comfort. She, too, pushed her dish back, indicating she'd finished.

'Then,' Nick paused, clearly unsettled, 'just a few weeks before your planned visit here, Cele called me.'

'What did she want?' Charles had said nothing until now, but was clearly curious about his cousin's love affair gone wrong.

'She said she wanted to see me. I agreed, but I was still a little uncomfortable about it. She said she had 'something of great importance' to tell me. I have to say: I was torn between curiosity and a feeling that I didn't really want to get involved in any of her problems. She was what you might call 'high maintenance.' I felt like I'd moved on. I didn't want to get drawn back into all her drama again.' He shook his head and laid his napkin down.

'But I didn't feel right refusing her. So we agreed to meet at a little diner we liked on Fisherman's Wharf. I wasn't looking forward to it much, expecting that she was either having marital problems, or experiencing some difficulty at the paper. Whatever it was, I couldn't see how I could help. But I felt I owed her at least the courtesy of listening, so I agreed.'

'And how did it go?' Gail prompted.

'Well, that's just it. The meeting never took place. *I* was there, on time. But she never showed up.'

'Maybe she changed her mind.' Connie suggested. 'Or perhaps the problem was solved and she felt a little foolish about contacting you.'

'I wish that'd been the case. A few days later Bobby called, plainly distraught. Cele's body had washed ashore somewhere down the coast.' Nick's voice had a catch in it. 'She'd been missing for a few days. Apparently, a local fisherman found the corpse. I have no idea what she was doing there, or whether she slipped, or jumped, or . . . ' He stopped, unable to continue.

Gail stared at Nick sympathetically. The death of an acquaintance was bad enough. But an untimely loss of someone you'd once known well was bound to be a blow. 'I'm so sorry, Nick, truly. What can we do to help?'

Connie nodded sympathetically and Charles reached across to pat his cousin's shoulder in support. Then the waiter brought the check, and they headed back to their hotel suite on Nob Hill.

★   ★   ★

Gail had rung for a bottle of wine, which now languished in an ice bucket near a small but elegant table overlooking the Bay, with much the same view as from the restaurant. Nothing else had been said about Nick's quandary, until finally he sighed long and loud: 'I'm not really sure what I'm asking for here.'

'Well, at least you should be able to get some answers from Cele's family about what happened to her. You deserve *that* much . . . ' Connie, true to his penchant for organization, had placed a yellow pad and several pens out on the table next to his wine glass.

'I suppose I could bluster my way in and demand some answers.' Nick shook his head in frustration. 'But I'm not under any illusions. I doubt Bobby, Jr. would be forthcoming. We butted heads a few times, and I'm sure he doesn't remember me with fondness. I don't even know her husband. I can imagine what he would think if one of Cele's old boyfriends showed up on his doorstep demanding an explanation about her death. No, I just don't see an opening in that direction. But . . . I'm just not happy leaving this as it is. There's something else there. I can feel it in my bones. Something's not right.'

Charles had been standing near the window. He wandered back and took a sip from the glass set aside for him. 'There *is* something we can do. Where was she found?'

'Down in Big Sur country — somewhere near Cliffside, I think. I'm not really familiar with that area. It was in the brief newspaper account.'

'Well, I can take a jaunt to whatever county processed the body, go through the records there, and see what turned up in the inquest. Those are supposed to be public records. There must have been some conclusion about the cause of death — they *did* hold an inquest, didn't they?' he said, turning to Nick.

'I honestly don't know. If they did, I never found it on-line. After the initial account in the *San Francisco Daily Press*, the only other announcement I could find was her mortuary notice. Absolutely nothing else. That's why I'm so puzzled. I did see Bobby, Jr. at the memorial service, but he refused to talk to me — said to get back to him later. But he hasn't returned any of my calls. And the husband, Timmy Lerner, wasn't even mentioned in the notice — and he didn't attend the service either. His old, rich parents were there — gad, they're everywhere in Bay Area society. So, what do I *do*, folks?'

'Give me a dollar,' Connie interrupted, holding his hand out to Nick.

Puzzled, Nick pulled out his wallet, fished out a bill, and handed it over.

Gail and Charles both smiled. They understood immediately. 'Now,' Connie said, as he slipped the greenback into his wallet, '*now*, Mr. Quintaine, you've just retained the firm of Osterlitz and Brevard to look into this matter for you. That means we can ask all kinds of people all kinds of questions, and go snooping about in all kinds of places — but we don't have to answer any questions about *you*. Lawyer-client privilege, you know.'

'Oh, yes, I see.' Nick looked chagrined. 'Of course, that'd be the most discreet way of handling it, I suppose. Seems like a lot of effort for what amounts to a rabid case of curiosity on my part. But yes,' he stood and raised his glass in turn to each of them, 'I hereby retain you to represent my interests in this matter!'

While they'd been talking, Charles had reached into his ever-present briefcase and pulled out his yellow pad. Gesturing to Connie, he raised his pen. 'OK, Boss, what's first?'

'Well, I think you had the right idea about the inquest. Why don't you take a run down the coast tomorrow and see what you can find. Check the local newspapers while you're at it. You never know what might turn up. It's possible the *Daily Press* kept the story out of the paper because of the family's influence here. Yes — ' He turned to a slack-jawed Nick. ' — Yes, it's still possible to keep things out of the newspapers and off the internet, even these days — *if* you know the right people.'

'But,' Gail broke in with a grin, '*ve have our vays*, don't we, guys? Anything you want me to do, Connie?'

'I was thinking — since Nick doesn't feel like raising his flag with the family, maybe he could give you a little background on Cele's Cal Berkeley days. Then you could call either the brother or the husband, saying that you were a classmate of hers. You were wondering if there was anything you could do to help. You know the drill.'

'Perfect, Nick,' she said, turning back to him. 'Can you give me a thumbnail sketch about your school days — classmates, professors, organizations? That sort of thing?'

'Sure, I'll see if I can pull together some material for you. I've also got some pictures stashed away. I could come back here for breakfast and go over them with you.'

'Good. Connie, what are you going to do?'

'I think I'll head out to the *World-News* offices tomorrow. See what I can dredge up there, not only about Cele, but also about her husband as well. Does anybody know what's happened to him?'

'Come to think of it, no,' Nick said, looking a little overwhelmed. 'I haven't seen anything about him in the press since, well, for at least a year. That's very odd, come to think of it. I wonder if he's gone undercover again. You sure you want to go to all this trouble, Gail . . . ?'

'Trouble?' Gail laughed out loud. 'Oh, Nick, you have no idea how much fun this is for us. This is what we *do*! You've just made our day!'

* * *

'Hello. Robert Burrell, Jr.? My name is Gail Brevard. You don't know me, but I was a friend of Cele's at school. I'm *so* sorry for your loss, but I just wanted to get some information for the *Alumni Newsletter* I edit.' Speaking into her cell phone, Gail was deliberately vague about *which* alumni. 'Do you have a moment?' She'd thought through her back story and had settled on the newsletter as a possible approach.

'Thank you, Ms. Brevard, is it? Yes, this has been a difficult time for us. What exactly did you want to know?' Bob Burrell's deep voice was polite but cautious.

'Oh, I didn't really want to *know* anything,' Gail gushed. 'But we try to keep a record of our former classmates — marriages, births, etc. And passings, of course. I just wanted to be sure I have her married name, dates, and all that, correct. I don't like to publish anything that's inaccurate. The thing is, I couldn't find an obituary for her in our local paper, and I just wondered if she'd been living in another area?'

'Yes, I see. Well, Cele had kept her maiden name. And as far as the *day* of her death goes, because of the circumstances . . . ' he gulped, then continued.

' . . . Because of the circumstances we only have an estimated date. Her husband's family asked us not to run an obituary — just a memorial notice — well, because of the child, you know. They thought that, in the long run, it'd be better if he didn't have all those awful details — you know, in later years.' He hesitated again. 'That certainly wasn't how *I* wanted to handle it, but out of respect for their feelings, I decided not to make an issue over it.' He stopped suddenly, as if aware he was speaking to a relative stranger and had, perhaps, said too much.

'Oh, I certainly understand,' Gail said hurriedly. 'We were all just devastated when we heard. Such a tragedy — with the baby and all. Well, these things happen. I just wish there was something I could do to help. Do you think her husband would be willing to talk to me? I mean, I don't want to be a nuisance, but Cele was such a friend to everyone at school. There are quite a few of us who were upset and concerned when we got the news.' She waited a beat. 'Of course, I do understand if you think he wouldn't want to be disturbed . . . '

'No, no, it's all right, it's just . . . ' Bob Burrell paused. 'The truth of the matter is that we've been somewhat estranged from Cele's husband and his family. The Lerners were not happy about the marriage . . . ' He stopped, now clearly concerned he'd once again gone too far. 'Well, that's all I'm going to say about this. I'm sorry, Ms. Brevard. I think you have enough information for your newsletter. I don't mean to be rude, but I have a business to run here.'

'I'm *very* sorry if I've kept you too long,' Gail said smoothly. 'And I really appreciate the time you gave me. As I said, my only concern was to properly record Cele's death for the newsletter. She had a lot of friends who will want to know about it. Again, my sincerest condolences to your family. I *truly* understand what a difficult time this has been for you. If you think of *anything*, anything at all I can do to help, please let me know.' She quickly gave him her number and broke the connection.

119

'Well,' she said to herself as she added to the notes on her pad, 'there's something nasty in the woodshed, I'll bet!'

* * *

Charles Walton tugged at his shirt collar as he sped south down U.S. Highway 101 in the shiny little red Mazda MX-5 he'd rented for his Bay Area stay. The early morning haze had burned off and it was a gorgeous day. There was a tinge of salt in the air and the brilliant sun beat down through the open windows. As he drove, Charles reviewed in his mind the details he'd jotted down about Cele's death — and the plan of action he had put together to discover what'd really happened to Nick's old flame.

He thought he'd begin his search at the Carmonte Public Library. Carmonte, although not the governmental seat of Santa Lucia County, was by far the largest town there. He'd search the local newspapers spanning a week's worth of dates on either side of the day her body was discovered, looking not just for Cele's name, but for any other incidents that might be related to the tragedy. Even if the San Francisco or Sacramento papers had squelched the story, it was more than likely that the Carmonte rag had commented on the death, if only in passing. Anything would be helpful. You never knew what might turn up as local gossip. It was worth the time it'd take to go through the papers, page by page. Searching on-line was fine as far as it went, but often the newspapers only posted a few days' worth of stories on their websites before dropping them. He'd already sifted through all the on-line material he could find. Even Cele's Wikipedia entry just recorded the date when her body had been discovered — but none of the circumstances surrounding it.

And if he couldn't locate anything in Carmonte, he'd head to the Santa Lucia County seat, the town of Salvaje.

As he pulled into Carmonte, he checked his GPS again to make sure he was on the right track. After a few fits and starts, he found the main library, parked in the city lot next door, and headed into a cool, Spanish-style courtyard. He paused a minute or two to take in the lovely old tile work and bubbling fountain, and watched a few children and their moms eating peanut butter sand-wiches and feeding several of the many birds gathered around what appeared to be a favorite watering hole.

'May I help you?' a pleasant young woman asked as he stopped at the reference desk just inside the door.

'Yes. I'm looking for local newspapers, hard copies if you have them, for a period of time spanning these dates.' He handed her a note with the information.

'Let's see,' the librarian said, examining his list. 'Yes, I think these will still be in the Reading Room. They haven't been sent out for filming yet.' She gave a floor chart of the library and noted the location for him.

'Thanks so much,' Charles said. He made a quick stop at the men's room and refreshed himself at the drinking fountain before heading off to the area the woman had indicated. There he sat in the sunny window, and systematically began looking for the newspapers he needed. With any luck, this stage would go quickly. He had a lot to do today, and the next phase, searching the Court House records in Salvaje, located sixteen miles to the northeast, would not be as straight-forward.

★　★　★

While Charles was heading south, Connie drove the eighty-seven miles east to Sacramento. The traffic was congested in the Bay Area, as always, but once he merged onto Interstate-80, things began flowing much more smoothly, and he made the trip in a record two hours.

The *World-News* Building was located in Sacramento just a few blocks from the California State Library, in a modern office complex that had replaced the old, four-story structure a decade earlier. The city seemed like a backwater community compared to the hustle and bustle of San Francisco, but he liked the broad, pleasant streets with their lines of trees, and enjoyed the absence of bumper-to-bumper traffic. He pulled into the underground parking structure, and took the elevator up to the second floor.

'I'm looking for Johnnie Wicks,' he said to the first person he encountered. He'd phoned on the way to make an appointment.

The woman pointed down an aisle, and said, 'Three rows down, fourth cubicle to the right.'

He spotted the reporter — a tall, graying man with a trim Van Dyke beard and the beginnings of a paunch — sitting in front of a computer, facing away from Connie.

'Your Majesty!' Osterlitz hollered, loud enough so that half a dozen of Wicks's neighbors swiveled around. Years earlier, the newspaper had run a humorous weekly column, touting the reporter as 'King of the Inland Empire,' complete with scepter and crown.

'Con, you old sourpuss, you!' Wicks responded, getting up and pumping the other's hand vigorously. 'Sonofagun, I wasn't expecting you quite so soon. Thought you'd be on the road another hour or two, at least. So, who are you threatening this time?!'

Osterlitz said with a grin: 'I'm out here on business — something else entirely — but I need to do a little local research on another matter, and thought you might be able to point me in the right direction. Or at least give me an idea of where to start.'

'Sure, I'll do whatever I can to help.'

Wicks had been at Stanford at the same time that Connie was getting his under-graduate degree there. The two were fraternity brothers, and had maintained a correspondence of sorts over the years. Although Johnnie had gone into journal-ism while Connie eventually had pursued his law degree, they had a lot in common, enjoying many a late-night debate over politics and current events in their younger years. Now, they exchanged Christmas cards and the like, but two hadn't actually met for several years. Connie hoped they still had enough in common that he could pull some of the details about Cele's mysterious death out of hiding.

'I, uh, wonder if there's any place more private where we could talk,' he said.

'That bad, huh?' Wicks smiled. 'If the conference room's open, we can use that. Let me check.' He picked up his phone, and spoke a few words. 'Yep, it's free. Follow me, my friend. You need a coffee fix?'

'Yes, please,' Connie said.

The two men stopped at the staff lounge, collected their drinks, and then headed down another hall. When they'd settled in the lush corner room with a panorama window overlooking part of downtown Sacramento, Wicks asked, 'What's up?'

'I'm trying to find out what happened to someone who worked here, for a client that was a friend of hers. I'll understand if your hands are tied, but I'd really appreciate anything you can tell me. Her name was Cele Burrell . . . '

'*Cele*? My God, of *course* I knew — and liked — her. It was terrible, just terrible, what happened.'

'Well, that's just it,' the attorney said. 'We're having trouble finding out what *did* happen to her. The details all seem to have been covered up by her family.'

★　★　★

Much later that afternoon, Gail made another call. 'Nick?' she said. 'We were hoping we could get together for dinner and share what we've found thus far. Charles should be back from Santa Lucia County by seven. The Court House down there closed at 4:30, and he's on his way north. Do you want to meet here at the Hotel?'

'Actually, there's a nice secluded place over in Ghirardelli Square we might try. Yeah, I know that's a bit touristy, but this place is actually off the beaten path, and quite good. It's a family-owned Italian-style restaurant. I think you'd enjoy it.' He gave her the name and address. 'See you at seven or so?'

'Sounds good.' Gail gave a thumbs-up to Connie, who'd just emerged from the shower. Then she hung up the phone.

'Shall we just have Charles meet us there?' she asked her beau.

'Yeah, that might be easier and quicker for him. I'm sure he'll be beat after spending all afternoon in the library, then fighting the traffic up the West Bay.' Connie grinned at her. 'Guess that gives us an hour or so, doesn't it?'

'Why, Mr. Osterlitz, is that a proposition?' Gail grinned back. 'My, my, my, whatever can we do to fill all that time . . . ?'

* * *

That evening, the four conspirators were seated around a comfortable leather booth in a back corner at Bella's, the *ristorante* Nick had described. He was a regular there, and the proprietors had given them a table out of the way where they could talk without being disturbed.

'Another piece of the puzzle,' as Gail described her discussion with Bobby Burrell. 'But he was definitely ill at ease. And there was certainly no love lost between him and Cele's husband. I think my next move will be to contact Timmy Lerner, and see what he has to say. I'll tell him that Cele's classmates would like to take up a collection for a memorial scholarship. See how that plays.'

'Well, you might have a little difficulty there,' Connie said. 'According to what Johnnie Wicks told me, Timmy and Cele were on the verge of splitting up.' Nick winced. 'Her so-called 'disappearance' was really a trial separation. Johnnie was friendly with Cele, and he claims that she'd confided to a few of her colleagues about the relationship. It seems that Mr. Lerner could be abusive, if not physically, at least mentally. Under the circum-stances, I doubt he'll be very responsive.'

'Does Wicks know how to get in touch with him — or his family? And who are these family members, by the way? His parents? Siblings? Bobby didn't really say.'

Nick spoke up. 'Lerner's parents are still living. And the baby, of course. I'm just supposing, but maybe they're the ones who're looking after the child these days. I don't know why, but I got that impression somehow.'

'Well, I could at least inquire about the baby. I suppose I could suggest that Cele's friends want to start a college fund for him. Maybe he'd be agreeable to that.' Gail pushed aside her salad and began on the ravioli.

'None of you have asked me yet how my day went,' Charles said. He crunched down on a bread stick. 'There *was* an inquest in Santa Lucia County.'

'Really?' Connie said. 'What conclusions did they draw?'

'That's just it: none. They never reached a verdict as to the precise cause of death. She had multiple cuts and fractures, including several to her head and neck — and any of several of them, alone or in combination, could have caused her passing. Sorry, Nick,' he added, when he saw his cousin's agitated expression.

'She didn't drown then?' Gail said. She took another sip of Chianti and laid down her fork. 'They can't just have signed off without stating a specific cause.'

'Yes, they can — and no, there wasn't any water in her lungs. I couldn't find an autopsy. Also, I have no idea what they did with the body. I think the family may have intervened directly, and suddenly swept the remains out from under the hands of the county authorities, perhaps with a major political donation under the table. I'm assuming this was Mr. Lerner, Sr., although no one will state that for the record. The Lerners have a great deal of clout in Northern California. The death certificate does say she was cremated, and was buried in the family vault.'

'But the coroner had to sign off before the body was released,' Connie pointed out.

'Well, if he did, his actual signature wasn't on the public record, like it's supposed to be. It's just a rubber stamp, and no one could tell me who 'stamped' the document. It also looks to me like they somehow got the records restricted. I'm not through with this, by any means; I'm just telling you what happened.' Charles wiped his mouth and sat back with a sigh. 'By the way, I did come across something in the newspapers down there that may be of interest. It has to be about Cele, although her name isn't mentioned.'

'What did it say?' Nick said, pushing away from his meal.

'According to a brief article that appeared a few days after the body was discovered, before a positive I.D. was made, she was found by an old fisherman who lived in a hut near the cliff.'

'We already knew that,' Gail said.

'Yes, but *here's* the interesting part: the piece says that he mentioned that he'd seen her a few days earlier, still alive, walking along the cliffs. He was certain that she'd been stopped by a blond man wearing a blue jacket or sweater. They appeared to argue briefly, then parted and went their different directions. He found her body a few days later, wedged in between some rocks at the bottom of the cliff. He claimed that it looked to him as if her neck had been broken — and he couldn't understand how her body could have been stuck so tightly in the rocks — by the tide, that is.' Charles looked at each one around the table.

'By the way: does anyone know if Timmy Lerner is blond?'

'I do,' said Connie. 'Wicks had some shots of Cele and her husband taken at a newspaper picnic, not long after their marriage. I believe his coloring was on the fair side, but I can't be absolutely sure without looking at them again. Johnnie is having some copies made for me, along with copies of society articles and such. Oh, by the way, the marriage announcement was very brief, and didn't include a formal portrait of the couple — as you probably already know, Nick.' Nick nodded. 'Which is a bit odd,' Connie continued, 'considering their positions and social status. There should have been something. What do you think?'

'I honestly don't know what to think — now.' Nick shook his head as if trying to clear the cobwebs. 'I don't know whether to leave this thing alone, or to try to find the truth. I just . . . '

'Look, why don't we sleep on it. We have a few more things we can do in the records, here and elsewhere. Then, after a few days, if you're uncomfortable with continuing, we'll just walk away.' Connie grabbed the check before Nick could make a move. 'We have a lot to consider. There may not be anything more to say about this — except that it's a terrible tragedy for the family.'

'I want to thank you all for your advice — and your care with this,' Nick said. 'My main concern is that she'd reached out to me and I wasn't there for her, when I could have been. I just want to be sure I did the right thing by her . . . ' His voice trailed off as he looked out into the night. 'I don't really think . . . '

'You did everything you possibly could,' Gail said, matter-of-factly. 'I think Connie is right. Let's give it a few more days and see what turns up. If we're satisfied by Friday that we've uncovered everything we possibly can, then I think you might want to give it a rest. After all, you have the Seymours, Aunt Nancy and Uncle Floyd, to handle. We need to get started on all sorts of new projects. I guarantee that will take your mind off this.'

'You're right, of course, as usual.' Nick

swigged the dregs of his wine. 'Now, I think we could all use a good night's sleep. Let's see what we turn up before the end of the week. Then I'll make a decision.'

But Gail was quiet as their cab sped back up the Hill to their hotel. And Connie knew her well enough to understand that the 'little gray cells' were chittering away. He smiled to himself. He'd bet the farm they'd still be in the City by the Bay come next week.

★   ★   ★

The next morning, bright and early, Gail called the hotel management and extended their suite and Charles's room 'indefinitely.' They were comfortable here and, depending on how their research progressed, might as well remain in the hotel for the duration. She also ordered in coffee, juice, and rolls. Connie, a night-owl by nature, was still sleeping, but she'd been going over things in her mind and now wanted to get her day organized.

'Charles?' She said into her phone

— she knew definitely that he too was a 'morning' person, so had no compunction about calling him early. 'Do you want to come by the suite before you head out? OK, see you in a few.' His room was located down the hall, and a short while later she heard a soft tap on the door. Room Service was heading toward them, so she stood there a moment to let the server — and Charles — in. Soon they were seated comfortably at a banquette in front of the window. This was going to be one of those gorgeous San Francisco days, filled with sunlight and fresh salty breezes. Gail and Charles exchanged happy smiles. They were in their element.

'Now, the first thing I'm going to do is try to find the elusive Mr. Lerner. I think Connie is planning an early lunch with Wicks in Sacramento. If I can get any kind of a meeting with Lerner, I'll try to draw him out about the so-called marital problems he and Cele were having. I'm also curious about his parents and the arrangements he's made for the child. Where are you headed?'

'I've got to go back to Santa Lucia

County. There's something not quite right about that inquest. I'm going to try and pull a few strings behind the scenes — see if I can talk to someone in the Coroner's Office in Salvaje. I'll file a writ if I must. There has to have been some kind of autopsy, I think. Also, we're still not certain about the disposal of the body, beyond the fact that it was cremated and taken away. And, if it's at all possible, I'm going to find that fisherman and interview him. If Connie or Nick can provide me with a photo of Lerner, Jr., I'll see if he recognizes him.'

Just then, Connie stuck his head out of the bedroom, gave a wave to Charles and mugged a kiss at Gail. 'Be out as soon as I dress. Don't drink up all the coffee!'

'Hurry up then, sleepyhead. Time waits for no man — or so I've been told!'

★   ★   ★

'What have you got for me?' Connie asked. He and Wicks had ordered lunch at a corner diner, The Partie-Civile, on 'J'

137

Street near the *World-News* Building in Sacramento.

'Well, first of all,' Wicks said, 'here are some photos I found, including a few casual ones taken at the company picnic earlier this spring.' He handed them over. 'But I think *these* will be more useful for you.' He pulled out a pair of 8 x 11-inch studio portraits, obviously of Cele and Timmy, probably submitted as part of their *C.V.*'s on file in the newspaper's Human Resources Department.

Connie looked them over carefully. Cele was not a classic beauty, but like Gail, there was something about her face that was very attractive. Her coloring was fair, but not blonde. Her hair was tousled about her face in a loose style that emphasized her femininity. Serious gray eyes, a straight nose, high prominent cheekbones, and an infectious smile spoke of intelligence, humor, and confidence. He would have liked to have known this woman. 'Lovely,' Connie said. Wicks nodded. Then he turned to its companion.

Timmy Lerner, the prize-winning crime

reporter, was dressed for the part. The Robert Redford look-alike boasted tousled blond hair draped over the side of his forehead; his piercing blue eyes gazed directly into the camera. A tweedy jacket was flung open revealing an open-necked checked sport shirt and a glint of gold — perhaps a chain. He would be attractive to the ladies, Connie had no doubt, but there was something — some basic gene — missing. Connie had seen, and known, enough 'players' in his time to distinguish the genuine from the phony. This one did not ring true.

'Know him well?' Connie indicated the photo of Timmy.

'Not really. We travel in different circles, if you get my drift,' Wicks said wryly.

'I think I do.' He took a sip of strong coffee and sighed. 'So you think he might have been abusive with Cele? Anything concrete? Any police reports — a restraining order perhaps?'

'Not that I'm aware of. Just that on several occasions Cele seemed particularly down. I can't exactly put my finger on it, but several of us who knew her thought that they'd argued, perhaps forcefully. I don't actually believe there was any physical violence — at least I saw no evidence of it. But you know as well as I do there can be other forms of abuse, every bit as destructive as the physical kind.'

'I certainly agree with you. And for someone of Cele's background and obvious gentility, verbal or psychological confrontations could have been even more devastating.' Connie shook his head sadly. 'What a shame. I just wonder how she really died. Do you think she was capable of taking her own life?'

'I would have said 'No,' except for one thing. When she left Lerner, she also left the baby with him. That doesn't sound like a young mother eager to get away from a bad marriage and start a new life, does it?'

'No, it doesn't. Have you found anything else?'

'Just these.' Wicks handed over a stack of newspaper printouts of the engagement announcement, coverage of the wedding itself, the honeymoon departure of the couple to Fiji, and the birth announcement for their only child.

'Interesting,' Connie said, flipping them over one by one. 'I don't recognize the setting.' He held up several shots of the marriage ceremony.

'Lerner, Sr.'s private estate near Napa,' Wicks said. 'My understanding was that these were the only shots released for public consumption — I think our coverage was actually much greater than in the S.F. paper. The older couple with the gray hair are the Lerners; the older woman with darker hair is Mrs. Burrell.'

'Hmm, that's interesting — the marriage took place on September 15th of last year, the child's birth on the following May 18th.'

'Yeah, Timmy was kidded about that unmercifully when the baby was born,' Wicks said. 'But a preemie isn't uncommon these days.'

'And Cele died about August 9th?'

'Something like that. This final clipping shows her funeral on the Napa estate ten days later.'

'I don't see her mother anywhere,' Connie noted.

'And Timmy isn't in any of these pictures either,' Wicks said. 'You have to realize, we were supplied these handful of shots by the Lerners; we couldn't get access to the estate itself.'

'Is that usual?'

'They're a pretty private bunch,' the newspaperman said. 'Mr. Lerner, Sr. keeps to himself these days. His wife is still involved in charity work, but not as much as before.'

'I mean, it's like Cele was *their* daughter, not Mrs. Burrell's,' Connie said.

'Go figure. Anyway, that's all I was able to find.'

'Well, I appreciate all your work on this. I owe you one.'

'Maybe two or three!' Wicks said.

Connie grabbed the check and gathered together the documents. 'You could do one more thing for me, Johnnie, if you would. Please fax copies of these materials to Gail at the Hotel. I don't know if Charles is underway yet, but if not, I think it would be helpful for him to have this portrait of Lerner — and if he has, she can text them to his cell phone.'

'If Charles has an app, I can send copies directly to him in his car.'

Connie nodded and handed Johnnie a card with their relevant numbers on it. 'There, that's the one he's using on the road.'

'OK, I'll get copies of everything over to the Hotel as well. Gail may need some of these materials today.' Connie had told Wicks of their various plans of attack. 'When you get to a breathing point in the next day or so, give me a call and we'll set up lunch or dinner for all of us. I'd like to meet Nick and Charles, and see Gail again, of course. That will be *my* pay for doing all this free research for you!'

'Deal,' said Connie. He shook Wicks's hand, left him to finish his coffee, and headed out the door.

★   ★   ★

'Hello, Mr. Lerner? You don't know me, but I'd like to have a moment of your time, if possible. My name is Gail Brevard, and I'm calling on behalf of some of your wife's friends who attended Berkeley with her.'

'What's this all about?' The gruff man's voice sounded impatient but curious.

'I wanted to express our sympathy with your loss but, more importantly . . . ' Gail continued hurriedly, hoping to fend off an abrupt disconnect. ' . . . More importantly, because we're aware Cele had recently given birth, I hoped I could tell you about a proposal we've gotten together — for the baby, that is.' She hesitated a moment, but there was no response.

'Several of us would like to 'pass it on,' so to speak, by organizing a scholarship program for Cele's child. In fact — ' Gail had a sudden inspiration. 'In fact, we're suggesting the scholarship be called simply 'Cele's Baby.' We could designate the funds to be set aside for him, whenever he's ready to continue his education, hopefully at Cal. What do you think?'

'Uh, I honestly don't have an opinion,'

Timmy Lerner said. 'You can do whatever you like.'

'Well, in that case, I suppose we'll just go ahead and get things set up — but still, we'll need the baby's full name, of course. Is he staying with you? I'd heard that perhaps your family was involved in his care — '

'Look Ms. Whatever-Your-Name-Is, I told you I don't really give a shit what you do. I can't stop you from doing it, but I can damn well keep you away from my child!'

'Oh, Mr. Lerner. I am so sorry to have upset you.' Gail tried to keep her voice low and on an even keel. She'd had plenty of experience dealing with angry witnesses, and her practice was to stay cool, calm, and collected. Often the other party would feel slightly embarrassed and eventually come around. You just had to keep them talking. 'I wouldn't have caused you any pain for the world. Really, we just wanted to express our sympathy and do something for the child. His future happiness is important to us — and we thought this would be a

145

positive thing we could do. But if you feel we're out of line . . . '

'No, no, I'm sorry I exploded that way, uh, Ms Brevard, is it? Sorry.' She could hear his choked sigh through the receiver. 'This has been a terrible ordeal for me and for my family. I'd like to make it up to you if possible. Why don't you meet me for coffee later today. I'll be free by then, and I'm truly sorry if I offended you. I was out of line.'

'Yes, I can do that. I'm in San Francisco. I assume you're at your office in Sacramento?'

'Well, actually, no,' he said. 'I've been helping my parents at their house in the Valley. We could meet in Napa at Julio César's Bisté, if you wish.'

'Shall we say around three? I should be able to get there by then.'

'That's fine. Just ask for me. I have a permanently reserved table there.'

Ah, Gail thought, the privileges of the rich and famous. She phoned Connie to relate her news, and suggested that he be present there, if possible, as a witness.

'Wonder why he was so touchy,' Gail added.

'Just try not to push any of his buttons. I don't want to have to come to your rescue. He looks like he's in pretty good shape, according to his picture, anyway.'

'Ah, my knight in shining armor. Run away! Run away!' Gail said, breaking the connection before Connie could respond.

But the smile on her lips was short-lived as she reviewed what they'd pieced together so far on the elusive Mr. Lerner and his even more elusive parents. And she wondered what Charles might be finding in Santa Lucia County as he tracked down the mysterious fisherman. Was Timmy Lerner the strange blond-haired man — the last person Cele spoke with before she plunged to her death off the cliffs?

*　*　*

Charles's main goal this gorgeous morning was to buttonhole someone — anyone — in the Santa Lucia County Coroner's Office, and try to get a few straight answers. There *had* to be some records on this unusual death, buried somewhere in the bowels of the system. He was like a bulldog when he got hold of something: he wouldn't let go until he reached bottom. As he drove south he considered once more the problem of the lone witness, the fisherman. *Why*, he wondered, was this person's testimony *not* on file (he'd found no evidence that the man had ever been questioned by the authorities). An eyewitness was too valuable a resource to dismiss so easily. There must be a problem with the man's story, or — and he hated to go down this road — or the truth of the matter might be that the Lerners had simply bought off the locals in some manner, and had swept their dirty laundry into the dust bin.

As he pulled off the main highway and entered Salvaje, the small county seat, he thought to himself: well, they had *him* to reckon with now. Nick and Charles were of an age, and because of the family relationship, he tended to look upon the younger man as a brother of sorts, particularly after the tragedy that had taken the life of another promising young woman, Floyd and Nancy Seymour's teenaged daughter, Vivian.

If there was anything he could do, anything at all, he was determined to uncover the truth behind Cele Burrell's untimely death. This was *his* family, now. And one of Charles's most attractive attributes was his loyalty — to Gail and Connie, who'd entrusted him with their business, but most of all, to his family — and Nick was an extension of that family. As he pulled into the Santa Lucia County complex, his jaw was set and there was steel in his gray eyes. Yessiree, they had Charles Walton to deal with today! Let the fireworks begin!

* * *

Later that afternoon, Gail met Timmy Lerner at Julio César's, a dinner house in the Napa Valley. By this time, Connie had driven west from Sacramento, and was already present when Lerner and Gail appeared.

The place was practically deserted at

149

mid-afternoon — in fact, the restaurant proper was partially closed, but the bar was always open, serving drinks, nuts, and light hors d'oeuvres. Connie gave Gail one of his trademark raised eyebrows, making sure that he could see Gail's face easily, so she could signal him if she sensed the interview was going wrong. She didn't respond, of course. After what Wicks had told him, he wasn't at all comfortable with Gail putting herself into harm's way. But at least he'd be near enough to step in (or call security) if Lerner made any direct threats against her. He sipped a cold Dos Equis and munched on the appetizers he'd ordered.

Gail was sipping on raspberry iced tea at a small table in the bar, when Timmy entered. He ordered a platter of the vegetarian egg rolls and fried wontons, and began wolfing them down. 'No time for lunch today,' he said by way of explanation. 'Do you want to go to my private room?'

'Not necessary for me,' she said. Gail wasn't particularly hungry, but it gave her something to do with her hands and, in her experience, a shared meal had a tendency to defuse certain situations. Lerner was an attractive, middle-aged man conservatively dressed in standard suit-and-tie. He said very little initially, but finally coughed slightly, drank a long gulp of lemon-flavored iced water, and said: 'Now, where were we?'

'First of all, let me apologize if I seemed out of line this morning,' she said. 'Really, Cele's friends and former schoolmates would just like to do something, anything at all, as an expression of our mutual loss. Many of us had not been in touch with her for some time, so it seemed doubly tragic that she had left a child who will grow up without having known what a wonderful person Cele was. We discussed this a bit, and it seemed as though the most meaningful way we could remember her — which would also benefit her son — would be to establish a scholarship in his name at our alma mater. I'm just asking you now if you or your family would have any objections — or if you would find this gesture at all offensive in any way.' Gail stopped, as if she was flustered and had run out of things to say. Truthfully, of course, she was watching Lerner closely to see how he would react to what she'd said — particularly about what a 'wonderful person' Cele had been.

Lerner thoughtfully stirred his coffee, loaded with several packets of sugar and creamer. To Gail, it seemed as if he was trying to come to some decision about her proposal, and was having a difficult time of it.

'If you'd prefer to take a few days to think this over, I'd be happy to meet with you again later . . . ' she offered hopefully.

'No, that won't be necessary. I honestly can't see any harm in this, although I'd want to run it by my father. It's just that this whole thing has been so terrible that we — my parents and I — decided initially not to publicize the details of Cele's death. We wanted to protect my — *our* child — from any future harm. That way, in later years, Nicholas wouldn't be subjected to the kinds of evil speculation that so often accompany these tragic events. As a reporter, I think I know a little bit about . . . '

'Nicholas?' Gail interrupted. 'Is that your son's name?'

'Yes. Actually, his full name is Timothy Nicholas Lerner, but we'd decided to call him Nicholas to avoid the obvious mix-up between him and me. It wasn't my choice, but, for some reason, Cele was adamant about that particular name, and I tried to accommodate her wishes.' He sighed and shook his head.

'It's, uh, lovely,' Gail said thoughtfully. A little bell had gone off in the back of her mind. 'I wonder where she got it.'

'Uh, I have no idea,' Timmy said, draining his glass and pushing it aside. 'Let me, uh, take care of this . . . ' he began, reaching for his wallet.

'Oh, no, there's no need. So,' she added, scribbling her signature on the ticket handed her by the waitress, 'so may I assume you have no objection if we establish some sort of a memorial scholarship for Nicholas?' She deliberately did not elaborate on the 'we.'

'I can't find any harm in it. Of course, you'll keep me informed of your progress?

Here's my card.' He left it on the table. 'You can reach me through the website if I'm away from the phone.'

'Thank you so much, Mr. Lerner. I do appreciate your time. I wonder if you wouldn't mind me asking where Cele was buried. Some of us would like to pay our respects.'

'Uh, she's in the Lerner family crypt at Saint Maxima's Cemetery.' A tear ran down his left cheek. 'I never even saw the body; it was too, uh, rough to, uh, you know, so Father had her cremated and brought back in an urn. He took care of everything down in Carmonte. Sorry, sorry, I just can't talk about this anymore.' And he fled in the direction of the restroom.

Gail tucked his card away in her wallet and nodded in Connie's direction; he paid his bill, got up, and left the restaurant.

Gail paused and went through her bag, as if she was looking for her makeup or a tissue. She waited a moment or two until Lerner emerged again and ran out the door. She followed him slowly out into the parking lot, and watched him drive away. Then she went over and got into the passenger side of Connie's vehicle.

'Well?' he asked, one eyebrow raised.

'He's agreed, in principle, to the scholarship. I didn't really give him much opportunity to squirm out of it. He seemed genuinely upset by his wife's death. Connie,' she added, a note of concern in her voice, 'what would you say if I told you that the child's name is Nicholas? And that Cele had insisted on that name? Does that ring any bells for you?'

'Hmm, I'd say it rings at least one. Let's just keep this bit of information to ourselves for as long as possible. No point in muddying the waters. Still — I'm not a big fan of coincidences — and this is definitely one of those.'

★ ★ ★

'Thanks for all your help,' Charles said, shaking the hand of the assistant he'd tracked down in the basement of the medical complex attached to the Coroner's

Office. 'This was exactly the information I needed.' He carefully stowed the copies of the autopsy report on Cele Burrell Lerner away in his briefcase.

'You're entirely welcome,' the assistant replied. 'Wondered why there weren't no more interest in these. Family wanted to keep it under wraps, I guess — no pun intended!'

Charles groaned inwardly, but managed a lopsided grin in response to the man's attempt at morgue humor. 'Well, guess I'll be on my way, then. You've got my number — in case anything else turns up. You know I'll make it worth your while.' He'd already rewarded the man substantially for 'finding' the missing records. He had no doubt he'd be the first to know if anything else came to light.

Charles hadn't bothered to review the paperwork extensively, beyond assuring himself that these were indeed the documents dealing with Cele's death. Plenty of time for that when he got back to the City. However, he still wanted to try to locate the missing witness. Glancing at his watch, he saw that it was a little after one. He had a tentative address, gleaned from the phone book back at the morgue. But unless the place was relatively easy to find, he might have to make another trip back here tomorrow. He hoped not. The long drive between Santa Lucia County and the City was beginning to get to him, in spite of his snappy little sports car and the beauty of the surroundings. Well, all he could do was try. He entered the street and number into the car's GPS system and was relieved to see a corresponding map pop up. He studied it carefully, then headed out toward the sea.

A half hour later, after a few false turns, Charles carefully edged down a two-lane oiled road pitted with holes that closely traversed the Cliffside area. He watched for any sign of a mailbox or house number on the sparsely scattered cottages perched precariously along the cliffs. He made several runs up and down the narrow byway and finally parked in a shady pull-out. He gathered a few items, including his cell phone, a mini tape-recorder, and a small notebook, got out, locked the car, and looked around to gather his bearings.

After consulting his watch again, he made his way gingerly to a tiny gray dwelling, pushed through a rickety wooden gate, and waded through long grass up to the porch to what was obviously the front door.

'Halloo?' he called out. He waited a moment then tapped tentatively on the rusty screen. There was no response. He sighed. The guy was probably out fishing or tending his traps. Maybe he'd have better luck at the back. The weeds were thicker here, and there were several small trees growing close to the house, their branches dipping menacingly, as if to ward off intruders. Nothing for it but to push his way through to the back door.

'Anybody home?' he called out again, but there was no response.

He headed down the path from the house toward the ocean — which he could see shining in the distance in the afternoon sun — but as he neared the edge, one rough tree branch suddenly snapped back in his face. He instinctively threw up an arm to prevent it from scratching him, but in the process, lost his footing and slipped forward on the muddy slope. 'What the . . . ?' he began, but never finished his thought. The mud gave way to gravel, the gravel to sandy loam. Charles realized, too late, that he'd inadvertently wandered onto the cliffside for which the area was named.

'Oh shit,' he thought, as he tumbled head over heels down the rocky tor. 'I'm done for!'

*   *   *

'We'd better call again,' Gail said, nervously peering out into the velvet night from their hotel window. 'It's not like Charles to be so late without letting us know. I'm afraid something's gone wrong.'

Connie nodded and reached for his phone again. He'd been trying to get through to Charles's cell phone for the last two hours, to no avail. Either he was out of the service area or . . . Connie tried not to think what else might have happened.

'Emergency Services? This is Conrad Osterlitz, an attorney. My partner, Charles Walton, was in Salvaje today, doing some research on the records at the local Coroner's Office for one of our cases. He failed to return to the City or to check in with us, which is totally out of character. I've been trying to reach his cell phone unsuccessfully for several hours. What do you suggest? Can you start a search for him from here — or do I need to contact the Santa Lucia County authorities? I'm very concerned.'

'You'll need to come down and file a MisPers, that is, a missing persons report,' said the detective at the other end of the line. 'Ordinarily, unless we suspect foul play, we wait seventy-two hours before initiating any kind of search for an adult unless, of course, he might be handicapped, either physically or mentally.' Connie indicated that was not the case. 'Well then, it might make more sense for you to go straight down to Salvaje yourself and file the report with the County Sheriff's Office there. In the meantime, you could call around to some of the hospitals in the area — there aren't many — to see if he's turned up in an accident. Do you know what kind of car he was driving?'

Connie referred to his notes. 'Yes, it's a red Mazda MX-5 convertible . . . license number 8IIK145 . . . a Hertz rental. He has GPS tracking capability installed. We should be able to get a location for the car, at least.'

As Connie was talking to the San Francisco authorities, Gail had called their P.I., Hugo Goldthwaite, back in Cathcart. 'Hugo?' she spoke urgently into the phone. 'We need you out — yesterday! Yeah. Charles went missing today while down in Salvaje researching a case for us.'

'How long's he been gone?'

'Just a few hours. But, Hugo, we can't raise him — at all. And you know Charles: that's just not like him. We're really concerned. Also — the case was a suspicious death — and he was trying to track down a witness today. You can understand why we're worried . . . '

'OK, let me get hold of Dad and then

call the airlines.' Hugo, Sr. was now semi-retired, but still kept a hand in the agency and could take over while Jr. was away. 'I'll get the first flight possible. Shall I fly into S.F.? Is that the easiest?'

'Yes, I'll arrange for a Hertz rental there. We're at the Nob Hill Hotel. Charles has a suite here, too, so I won't bother to book you in. You can bunk in his room for the time being, at least until we know what's happened to him. Thanks, Hugo. Sorry to push this on you, but I think we're going to need 'all hands on deck' here.'

'You bet. I'll hold a good thought for Charles. I'll call once I get to the airport, so you'll have an idea about when to expect me. And Gail . . . ?'

'Yes?'

'Hang in there. Charles is one smart cookie. I'm sure he'll be OK.'

'I know. But we have no idea what's happened. This is just so unlike him. Have a safe trip.'

She rang off just in time to open the door for Nick, who peered anxiously into

162

her face as he entered the room. 'Any news?'

'None. I was just talking to Hugo. I asked him to come out. Even if Charles turns up, I'm beginning to think we could use the extra help. Nick, I'm convinced there's more to this story than just a tragic accident. Do you still want to pursue the inquiry?'

'More than ever, now.' He shook his head violently. 'If anything's happened to Charles, I'll never forgive myself. But I feel that I must get to the bottom of this. There's a mystery here. And, with your help, we can solve it.'

★   ★   ★

Charles's first sensation upon regaining consciousness was of leaf-filtered light playing across the clean, brightly-colored quilt which covered most of his body. He turned his head slightly to find the source of the light — then grimaced at the sharp pain.

'Oww!' he muttered under his breath.

'It would be best if you didn't move too

quickly,' a steady voice said nearby. 'It is not known yet how much damage there is. Here,' and a strong arm raised his head slightly and held a cup to his lips. Charles gulped the cold water gratefully. 'That is enough. You should rest now.'

'But — ?'

'No, you must rest. Time enough to talk later.'

Charles sank back onto the pillow, closed his eyes, and went back to sleep. Yes — time enough later to talk.

★ ★ ★

'Sorry to hear about all this,' Wicks said, as he took a seat at the table in the Nob Hill Hotel coffee shop the next morning. He'd just driven in from Sacramento. 'Let me know what I can do.'

'Johnnie — thanks so much for joining us. First of all, you remember Gail, don't you?' Wicks leaned over and gave her a quick peck on the cheek. 'And these are our colleagues, Nick Quintaine and Hugo Goldthwaite. Nick is Charles's cousin, as well, so I know he's doubly concerned.'

'Anything I can do. If you need me to call in some favors with the authorities . . . or with the paper. I can get a story in tomorrow's morning edition, if you think that would help.'

'I'm not sure what's the best thing here. If he's had an accident, then we need to get everyone down there looking for him. But if he's being held against his will for some reason, well, I just don't know. What do you think?'

'When we've had something like this in the past, a kidnapping or mysterious disappearance of some sort, we've tried to accommodate the authorities as closely as possible. Do you have anyone specific working with you?'

'I've talked to several people — including a Detective Ramírez here in San Francisco . . . '

Wicks nodded. 'Yes, I've heard of Juan: he's a good man, although I don't know him personally.'

' . . . And I've talked to two or three people in Salvaje. They're reluctant to do much before that blasted seventy-two-hour prohibition is up. The problem is, we all know Charles too well. This is totally unlike him. And, of course, there's Cele's suspicious death at the heart of all this . . . '

'Let me call Ramírez, and see if I can't get him started on this before the seventy-two hours have elapsed. We can give it till tomorrow. If we have nothing by then, I think we should go public, if not with the Cele Burrell connection, then at least the fact that a responsible person has gone suspiciously missing. Of course, it's always possible he went off the road somewhere and just hasn't been spotted. I think Hugo should take a run down the coast as quickly as possible and start backtracking his movements. *Someone* must have seen him.'

'I'll drive down this afternoon,' Hugo said. He'd only been in San Francisco a few hours, having arrived in the middle of the night. He was exhausted, but was accustomed to working on adrenaline. He checked all the pertinent numbers and the license plate with Connie, gave Gail a thumbs-up, and headed out. 'I should probably book a room there for tonight.

Just in case,' he added.

'I feel so damned helpless,' Gail said, staring into the dregs of her coffee. She'd drunk so much of it by now that she felt giddy and on edge. 'Wish there was something more I could do.'

'I feel the same way, but I can't think of anything right now,' Connie admitted. 'I suggest you get some rest, Nick. There's absolutely nothing we can do until we hear something. And I'll keep checking with people, including Hugo. If I hear anything, anything at all, I'll call you immediately.'

Nick thought a moment, then admitted he was beat. 'But instead of going all the way back to my place, I think I'll just crash in Charles's room — if that's all right,' he said. Gail and Connie both nodded. 'Please, don't hesitate to wake me if you hear anything.'

'I will,' Connie said, handing Nick a duplicate key card. 'Get as much rest as you can.'

Wicks got up, gulping the last of his iced tea. 'I'm heading back to my office. I'll try to phone Ramírez and emphasize the seriousness of all this, but he doesn't really know me, so I'm not sure how effective I'll be. Sometimes, though, when the police realize the press is taking an interest, it has an amazing effect on people. Suddenly they can move mountains. I'll call you if I hear anything on my end.'

Gail and Connie then headed up to their suite. Once Gail had snuggled down under the covers in the dimmed bedroom and began to doze, Connie moved back out to the living area and got out his notes. Maybe if he went over things again some of this would start to make sense.

Just then his phone quivered. He quickly punched 'Talk' and gave his name.

'Mr. Osterlitz? This is Deputy Bart Singleton, in the Santa Lucia County Sheriff's Office, calling about the missing person you reported. We've found the car. But there was no one inside. No, it didn't look as if it had been damaged. And your friend? He's still missing.'

*   *   *

'Hugo?' Connie's voice was rough from all the talking he'd been doing. 'You need to check in with the Santa Lucia County Sheriff's Office, right away. A Deputy Singleton.' He listened a moment to Hugo's response. 'Yes, they've found the car, but no Charles. Maybe you can figure out from the location where he might be. I've given them as much information as I thought they needed, without compromising our own investigation, of course. But I'd be more comfortable if you were looking over their shoulders. I told them you'd be contacting them as our legal representative.'

'I've checked into the Cliffside Lodge,' Hugo said, 'and was just about to head out. I'll stop at the Sheriff's Office first and see what they have. If I can get a specific location on the car, I'll fan out from there and canvass the locals. Someone had to have seen him. I'll call you if anything turns up — you do the same.' Hugo rang off and Connie roused Gail from her nap.

'You're sure they said there had been no damage to the car? Could they tell if his things were still in it?' Gail said.

169

'Of course, they didn't know what he had with him, but I've given Hugo a complete inventory of what I thought he took today. If his phone and briefcase are gone, he may have taken them with him, if he headed out on foot, that is. Can't think why he would do that — unless — ' He grabbed his phone again and began punching in numbers.

'Deputy Singleton? This is Connie Osterlitz again. I just remembered something. I believe Mr. Walton may have been looking for a local man, an old fisherman who lives in the Cliffside area. No, sorry, I don't know his name, but he apparently had discovered the body of a young woman near his house on the cliffs a short time ago. Yes, that's the one. If you have an address for him, that may be where Mr. Walton was headed.'

'Yes sir,' the Sheriff's deputy said. 'We'll get right on it. Your operative, Mr. Goldthwaite, is with me now. I'll include him in on this, I assume?'

Connie assured the detective that Hugo should be briefed on whatever operations the department was conducting in the matter of the disappearance of Charles Walton, and then rang off.

'OK, Hugo's there, so at least we're covered. God, I hope Charles is all right.'

Just then there was a tap at the door and Nick stuck in his head.

'Good news, Nick,' Connie said, making note of Nick's anxious expression. Then he briefed his friend on the most recent developments. 'I'm relieved there was no damage to the car. I suspect we'll hear something shortly.'

Gail called Wicks to let him know the news, and suggested he hold off on any story until they had more to report. Then they sat down to wait. The moments passed slowly, turning into one hour, then two. Just as they were about to leave for the dining room, Connie's phone buzzed once more.

'Yes, any news? I see. All right. I'll be there as quickly as possible. Thanks for letting me know.'

'What?' Gail and Nick spoke in unison.

'Sit down and I'll tell you what they found . . . '

The second time Charles came around, his head was a little clearer and the pain was not quite as sharp. The sunlight from earlier in the day (*was* it the same day?) had faded completely, and he realized that the tiny wood-framed room where he lay on a comfortable bunk, still wrapped like a mummy in the brightly colored quilt, had been lit by a dozen waxy tapers. The flickering glow was soothing, and other than the fact that he didn't know where he was or what had happened to him, he felt at ease. He suspected that the nagging doubts at the back of his brain would push forward at some point and encroach upon this idyllic hiatus, but until then, he chose to just relax and wait for further enlightenment.

'You feel better now!' The strong male voice emanated from the foot of the cot. Charles directed his gaze there to discover a slim, straight figure, like a stone god, perched on a rustic, three-legged stool.

'Yes, thank you very much for rescuing me,' Charles said, trying to recall the sequence of events which had led him here. 'I think I tripped or missed my footing somehow. I hope I wasn't too much trouble.'

'No, you were fortunate to have fallen exactly where you did. Otherwise . . . ' The figure shrugged impassively, Buddha-like, and made a motion with his hand. ' . . . Otherwise the outcome might not have been as happy.'

'Yes, I expect you're right. Please, do you have a phone? I need to call my friends and let them know I'm all right.'

'Sorry, but I have no telephone here. No lines, you see. And I don't think your other device . . . ' he indicated Charles's cell phone and notebook, laid out carefully beside him on the table next to the bed, 'I don't think it will be serviceable either.'

'I must get hold of them, though. You do understand? They'll be worried about me . . . ' Charles didn't know if this person would want to be involved with the police, but at least he could warn him of the possibility.

'Perhaps I could walk out to the main

highway. There is a general store. I could call someone for you from there. I would have done so before now, but I didn't want to leave you alone.'

'Of course, I'm grateful for what you've done. But now I need to get word to my friends. How long is the walk to the highway?'

'Perhaps twenty minutes — half an hour — no more than that. If you're feeling better by now, I can . . . '

But just then there was the chatter of a low-flying helicopter. Broad swooping lights flashed back and forth across the window, momentarily lighting up the room like day, then allowing it to fade back into semi-darkness as the chopper moved on. A muffled voice amplified by loudspeaker could be heard, echoing back and forth across the cliffs: 'Mr. Walton. Mr. *Charles* Walton. Can you hear us? Please show yourself.'

'*There!*' Charles moved suddenly and blinding pain forced him back against the pillow. 'That's me!' he groaned to the slight figure rising across from him. 'Please! Please let them know I'm here!'

Silently his benefactor stood and shuffled slowly out of the tiny room. Charles could only pray that he wasn't too late, that the old man would be able to signal the search party so they could come to his rescue. After all, he thought suddenly, he still didn't know exactly what role the fisherman might have played in Cele Burrell's untimely death. Would he ever know? And, more importantly for him, would he ever see his friends again?

★　★　★

'Take it easy, buddy.' Hugo's strong arms lifted Charles like a rag doll and deposited him carefully on the waiting gurney. It had been a struggle, getting the ambulance paraphernalia and crew inside the fisherman's hut, but they'd finally succeeded, judicially moving the old man's meager furnishings about until they could make a clear path to the tiny sleeping room where Charles lay. 'I've got you. Just hold on a bit longer and you'll be right as rain.'

Charles choked back tears of joy and relief at seeing his old friend. Once he knew Hugo was part of the rescue team, he finally relaxed and just allowed them to push and pull him about. Hugo was here! It was amazing how much small truths could be so relished when you were in the midst of an emergency. He had to hold himself in check to keep from plopping a huge wet kiss on the P.I.'s cheek. He snickered, knowing how the man would respond to such a thing. Still, he couldn't remember the last time he'd been so relieved, so happy, so thankful for small favors.

'Hugo,' he said, as they began making their way through to the door. 'Please — please,' he emphasized, as Hugo bent close to hear him. 'Please be sure to take care of the old man. He saved my life, you know. He *literally* saved my life. He's the witness we need for the case. Don't lose track of him — and take care of him — you know what I mean?' The pleading in Charles's eyes and voice was palpable, and moved Hugo more than he would have thought possible.

'Don't worry about a thing, buddy: I've got it covered. I have his name and mailing address, and I've made note of the location here in my GPS. I also tucked a C note in his pocket, and once we get back to the City, I'm sure Connie will increase that significantly. All you have to worry about now is getting better. We'll take care of everything else.'

As the medivac chopper took off into the darkness, heading back to the Santa Lucia County Trauma Center, a lone figure stood silently watching from the cliffs. He patted his shirt pocket and, for the first time during the long day, he smiled slightly. A very long time ago, he'd embraced the Buddhist philosophy to save himself from the afterimages he still carried within his seared soul of the carnage in Vietnam. Karma was all-powerful, he'd learned. You cannot fight karma. It would be like fighting yourself. The chain of events that had been put into play not so long ago, when he first had noticed the sad young woman making her painful way across the cliffs, had finally come full circle. He made the same hand gesture he had made earlier to the man who was named Charles.

'So be it,' he said to himself. 'All is well.'

* * *

'So what's the prognosis?' Gail had asked anxiously. 'Will he be all right?'

'Well, it's 'early days,' as they say, but yes, I think we safely can predict a full and complete recovery for Mr. Walton.' The physician who was in charge of the Santa Lucia County Trauma Center's ER facility in Carmonte had directed Gail and her friends to the family waiting area, where they nervously perched about the room. Connie was pacing impatiently back and forth, while Nick and Gail just huddled together, discussing various aspects of the Burrell case, and Hugo dozed in his seat nearby.

Gail could recall little of their mad dash down the coast, once they'd received confirmation of Charles's safe rescue. Connie had put his foot to the floor-board. Once they'd hit the Trauma

Center, he'd bulldozed his way past the nurses' station and the security guards with an intensity Gail had rarely seen in him.

'You see,' she whispered to Nick, as they ran to keep up, 'I think he feels so responsible for what happened to Charles. And I think he's also recalling how *he* felt, when he was in a similar situation down at Black Bear Lake . . . '

Now, as they huddled together, Gail's red tresses contrasting with Nick's dark hair, she retold the story of the murder case she and Connie had solved, with Charles and Hugo's help, during their *last* vacation.

'I guess we're just doomed if we try to get away from home for a little rest and relaxation,' she deadpanned. 'I can't say we don't ask for it, but sometimes I wonder if we aren't tempting fate a little too much.'

'Well, I don't know why Connie should feel responsible. If there's any blame to go around, I should get the lion's share. After all,' Nick grimaced in remorse, 'all this was because of me . . . and my blasted curiosity. Just couldn't leave the thing alone, could I?'

Gail patted his shoulder sympathetically. 'There's no need to beat yourself up, Nick. We all jumped in with little or no urging required. So if there's any blame, we share it. Besides, this is the kind of thing that could have happened anytime, anywhere. Charles was just lucky that old man found him when he did. Cele wasn't as fortunate, I guess.'

'You're right, of course, you always are,' Nick gave her a lopsided grin. 'From day one, you've always had a pretty good take on things. I need to pay more attention to your advice.'

'Can I get you two coffee or anything else?' Connie interrupted. 'I'm going nuts just moping around here, so I think I'll head down the hall and see if I can find a dispenser.'

'Hang on, I'll go with you,' Nick got up quickly. 'I think I spotted something as we were coming in. Coffee, Gail?'

'No, thank you. I'm just numb at this point, and if I drink any more coffee I'm going to turn into a wet pile of

Colombian beans! Don't bother getting anything for Hugo, either. I think it's going to take a bulldozer to get him up!' She gestured over at the gently snoring P.I., slumped down in one of the larger lounge chairs.

As Connie and Nick headed out of the waiting room and down the hall, Gail wandered over to the broad plate glass windows overlooking the parking lot. She watched silently a bit, as ambulances came and went, their lights ablaze and sirens blaring. Then she turned back into the room and took her seat again. Her brow was furrowed and her jaw set, as she pondered the moral dilemma in front of her. She had a decision to make — and it wasn't going to be an easy one.

* * *

'We're all relieved at the good outcome, Con,' Wicks said over the phone. 'It too often goes the other way. In our business, we often see more unhappy resolutions than happy ones, y'know? I'm just elated how this one turned out.'

'Me, too, Johnnie,' Connie said. 'And, even more importantly, it looks as though Charles's injuries weren't as serious as we first thought. He's got quite a bit of pain, of course, from that broken collar bone, but, all in all, he was one lucky guy.'

'Yeah, I can't help but think that Cele's fall may have been a similar situation — same area and all. Except, of course, for those anomalies you've pointed out — and the fact no one found her in time. Those worry me . . . '

'The key's that old man,' Connie said. 'You know, the witness? — the one who was the last person, apparently, to see Cele alive.'

'I wonder what really happened,' Wicks said.

'Well, I do think we're closer to the truth now. We're making plans to eventually bring the old fisherman into the City. Treat him to a day on the town, but also depose him — legally, I mean — just in case we end up in court over all this. Of course, a lot will also depend on what Nick decides to do. He's going to have some tough decisions to make, I think, if we're going to get to the bottom of this affair.'

'Just keep me in the loop. You know I'll be glad to testify, or provide archives or the other information available to me. I thought a great deal of Cele. She was a decent person, and would have made a fine newspaperwoman one day, if she'd had the chance. If there *was* anything sinister about her death, I'll be ready, willing, and able to lend a hand.'

'Thanks, Johnnie. You've already been a great help, morally as well as materially. It's always nice to have a real professional in your corner, as well as a true friend. I just hope I can repay the favor some day. I bet there are a bunch of newspaper conferences in my neck of the woods. You know, you always have a place to stay . . . '

'I might take you up on that,' Wicks said. 'There's something coming up next spring . . . '

★   ★   ★

'How would y'all like to go on a picnic?' Connie stretched and held out his hands toward the warm sun streaming in through the hotel window. The 'Fabulous Five,' as Gail had dubbed them, had gathered for an early morning breakfast around the banquette table in their main suite. Gail set down her coffee cup and looked quizzically at her mate.

'That would be a first,' she said dryly. Connie was known for enjoying his comfort. He was *not* an 'outdoors' person, by any measure, and she couldn't recall, in the half dozen years or so they had been together, that he *ever* had expressed such a desire, which was all right with her, considering her natural clumsiness. She wasn't an 'outdoors' person, either!

'A picnic along the cliffs south of Carmonte,' he added innocently, as if she hadn't spoken at all. 'I still have a few unanswered questions, and I'll bet the rest of you do, too. How better to do a recon of the area, then by plunking down seaside with a few sandwiches, a jug of wine, and thou?'

'I've been thinking the same thing myself,' offered Hugo. 'Not the picnic thing, I mean — but I'd really like to eyeball the scene of the 'accident.' I sure hate to leave this puzzle with all these doubts.'

Charles rolled his eyes. He was feeling much better now, and had been released for recuperation, with strict warnings to 'take it easy.' He'd been doing just that, holed up in his hotel room, bunking with Hugo, who was fetching and carrying for him. 'I think that would be against doctor's orders for me,' he said, somewhat petulantly. 'But the rest of you should feel free — '

'Nonsense,' said Gail, ever the practical one. 'They said nothing about you taking short car rides, and there's no reason we couldn't settle you safely somewhere there out of harm's way while we have a look around. *Ooh!* I've got an idea . . . '

'What's that?' all of the men echoed at the same time. Gail was always full of ideas.

'Well, what if Charles paid a visit to our fisherman friend, Mr. Maleta? You know you've been wanting to pay your respects,' she said, turning to Charles. 'We could settle you there, at the hut — maybe set up our picnic lunch nearby — then we, the rest of us I mean, could go look at the accident site, while you have a visit with your rescuer. Does that sound like a plan?'

'Sounds good to me,' piped up Nick. He'd been in much better spirits since Charles's safe return. 'I think we need to be very careful, though. Check everything out with the authorities first. I don't want anyone else taking a tumble.'

'Of course. I can get hold of Deputy Singleton later this afternoon,' said Connie eagerly. 'Get some suggestions and their permission to look at the site, at least let them know our plans. In the meantime, Charles can try contacting Mr. Maleta through his friends at the grocery store. I don't think he goes anywhere, other than out to check his traps and lines, so I suspect he'll be available. You think of anything else we need to do?' He'd already begun scribbling a list on his ever-present yellow pad.

'I'll talk to the hotel kitchen staff — see if they can provide us with all the fixings for a first-class meal,' Gail offered. She smiled happily. This was beginning to sound like fun. 'Gee, I'm glad you thought of this,' she said to Connie. 'Can't think of a better way to spend an afternoon!'

'I'll get my van all gassed up and outfitted comfortably in the back for Charles,' offered Nick. 'Plus safety gear, blankets, pillows, and the like. You'll be snug as the proverbial bug in a rug, *'Chuckie.''* He grinned evilly at his cousin. Gail suddenly realized that Nick knew full well how much Charles hated his nickname, and that his continued use of it was just an innocent form of 'sibling' rivalry, Charles being the closest thing to a brother that Nick had ever had.

'All right, you up for this, Charles?'

Charles nodded gamely. If he'd any doubts at all, he wasn't about to burst their pretty bubble. And it *would* be nice to see the old gentleman who had taken such thoughtful care of him again. 'You know, I never *did* get a chance to interview the fisherman properly — about what he saw that day, I mean,' he said. 'I believe I'll take my tape recorder and see if I can get the full story from him.'

'That's a good idea. Hugo — can you think of anything else we might need?'

'Plenty of sunscreen, Boss — plenty of sunscreen for us pasty-faced city-slickers!'

★ ★ ★

The next day dawned slightly overcast, which put a damper on the planned expedition. But after an hour or so, as they were still gathering what necessities they'd decided to take, the sun gradually began to work its way through the haze, promising warmer temperatures and a pleasant aspect overall.

Gail, clad in jeans, t-shirt, and hiking boots, was well-prepared with layers of sweaters and windbreakers, not to mention extra socks galore. Knowing her well-documented tendency to feel the cold a lot more than anyone else around her, she wasn't about to be caught without some manner of staying comfortable. For additional protection, she added small packets she had found at the Hotel

Gift Shop, which included a folded-up rain poncho and a light-weight collapsible umbrella. Her large canvas tote also contained her ID and hospital card, cell phone (although she'd been warned repeatedly it wouldn't operate out on the cliffs), a small notebook, and a digital camera with extra batteries, not to mention a water bottle, power bars, lip balm, her cosmetic pouch, a tiny hair brush, and a scarf. As she looked through her treasures for the umpteenth time, Connie raised his eyebrows (both of them) in mock exasperation.

'We're not crossing the Sahara, Gail,' he said, amused by her due diligence. 'We'll only be there a few hours, at most. And everyone, including the Sheriff's Department, knows exactly where we'll be. What can possibly go wrong?'

'What indeed?' Charles broke in wryly, gesturing with his good hand toward his still-bandaged collar bone. 'Ah yes, my friend. What could *possibly* go wrong?'

Connie shrugged and turned away to count his own treasures, secured tightly in a small, heavy-duty backpack. He wanted both hands free, in case he needed to do any serious climbing or grabbing.

Nick and Hugo were already waiting in the garage. They were both traveling light, having had a little more experience in such matters, and had volunteered to get the van gassed up and ready.

Gail, Connie, and Charles took one more reluctant look around their safe haven, then headed out. They made one detour, to the coffee shop, where a huge, lavishly-prepared picnic basket with cold packs awaited them.

They made their way out of the restaurant, Connie struggling under the weight of the basket.

'All right, let's see if we can find Peck's Bad Boys before they get into too much mischief.' Gail led their group in the direction of the garage. 'Hopefully, the rest of this trek will be as smooth.'

*   *   *

'Welcome,' the elderly fisherman bowed to their party. 'Please — make yourselves comfortable.' He was a short, wiry man with rough, dark, weathered skin from years spent in the sun.

The fickle sun had finally made up its mind to cooperate, and the day had turned into a dazzling delight. The further south they went, toward the sea, the prettier and more moderate the day had become. By the time they'd reached their destination, halfway down Cliffside Lane, and pulled into the shady enclave near Mr. Maleta's humble dwelling, they were glad of the cooling breezes and filtered light touching here and there in the tall grass.

From this perspective, and with a much less critical eye than before, Charles felt an almost nostalgic leap in his throat as he gazed about him at the quiet rural surroundings. Instead of run-down and ramshackle, the small Maleta homestead now seemed to him to be a lovely spot indeed, with wild ramblers twining about the porch railing, bees flitting from blossom to blossom in an ecstasy of glut, and multitudinous birds of all kinds, calling to each other from the lofty treetops surrounding the property. This was a paradise of sorts, he recognized, much to his chagrin. He had misjudged the place entirely during his earlier, cursory exploration. Today he wanted only to lie back among the grasses, sniff the salty breeze, and explore the meaning of life with his new-found friend. He contented himself now to watch Gail, under Mr. Maleta's serene guidance, spreading out the lovely repast on blankets under the trees.

'Come on, now,' she called to her brood, and also nodding to the fisherman. 'It's all ready!'

'Great! I'm starving!' Hugo plunked down in a soft shady spot. 'What's to eat?'

Gail poked about in the cavernous basket. 'Sandwiches — plenty of sandwiches — tuna, ham and cheese, roast beef.' She happily began putting together plates of goodies and passing them out among the hungry crew. In the meantime, Mr. Maleta had set up a rustic old table in the shade of the tree, where several large pitchers of cold tea and lemonade reposed. Connie stocked their cups with ice from the chest in the back of Nick's van, and prepped several bottles of California wine gleaned from the wineries in the Napa Valley.

Charles was deposited out of the sun on a pile of cozy comforters and plumped up pillows, and Gail brought over a plate of food on the makeshift tray provided by Mr. Maleta. 'Everything OK, Your Highness?' she joked.

'My minions have provided all my wants,' Charles deadpanned back. 'Get on with 'ee, wench! I have no further need of 'ee!'

Laughing, Gail plunked herself down next to Connie and began on her own plate in earnest. Between courses, the healthy members of the crew began to look over Hugo's detailed maps and, with some judicious advice from Mr. Maleta about tackling the steep path down to the shoreline, decided on their course of action. The fisherman ate sparingly from the vegan selections.

Nick and Hugo, as the two most physically adept members of their group, would scout the trail ahead for obvious pitfalls on their slippery slope. Gail would come next, with GPS, maps, and a tiny digital camera in hand, and Connie would bring up the rear, with a lengthy rope and first aid kit in his back pack. All four carried working walkie-talkies set to the same channel, a small flashlight, matches, water bottle, and leather gloves. Hugo had a collapsible shovel strapped to his back, and Nick an emergency band radio in his pocket. Charles, remaining behind with Mr. Maleta, would have his own walkie-talkie to monitor their progress.

'Overkill,' Hugo pronounced, looking on with amusement as his companions prepped for their assault on the cliff, but Connie just shrugged.

'Better safe than sorry,' was his laconic response. 'Are we ready?' he added, looking around with satisfaction. 'Let's get the show on the road.'

As the intrepid four headed off to find the trail to the beach, Charles switched on his tape recorder and began to interview Mr. Maleta about the events leading up to Cele's demise. He hoped, even if no new information was retrieved, that something the old gentleman would remember during their conversation would shed some light on the sequence of events. In particular, he wanted to gain more details about the mysterious blond-haired man. He'd brought along copies of the studio portraits of Cele Burrell and Timmy Lerner, just in case Maleta could identify them. The fisherman had said that he'd been too far away to make a positive ID of the man (one of the reasons, supposedly, he hadn't been subpoenaed for the brief inquest), and wasn't even sure of the woman until she'd turned up dead on the rocks a few days later.

'Too far,' he said again today. 'They were too far for these old eyes to see clearly.'

Still, Charles was an optimist at heart. If there was any possibility of clarifying the situation, he was going to give it his all.

* * *

'Careful!' Connie called to Gail, as she gingerly made her way down the slippery shale slope in front of them. 'This stuff can be treacherous.'

They'd first examined the scuffed area on the cliff top from which Cele had fallen from, but there were too many tracks of emergency and other personnel there for them to make any sense of the scene. Now they were heading down the cliff to the bottom.

'I know, I'm trying . . . ' The one bone of contention between them was Connie's eternal tendency to micromanage *everything* — including how Gail got herself from one place to another. Of course, that's what made him such a good lawyer, she reasoned: his thoroughness and insistence on detail.

The midday sun was hot now, beating down on them without mercy, and she paused just a moment to get her breath and her bearings, and to take in the magnificent scenery. Then, blowing a wisp of hair out of her eyes, she slogged on, acutely aware of Connie's slip-sliding, heavy-footed tread behind her. She'd lost sight of Nick and Hugo, who'd bounded on ahead like a pair of mountain goats. Oh well, she thought wickedly, at least she had the maps with her. They'd probably have to stop at some point and wait for her, just to find out where they were!

At last Gail, with Connie close on her heels, clunked down on a huge rock jutting out of the sandy shoreline at the bottom of the cliffs. She brought out the tiny camera and shot several scenic views, then aimed it back up the narrow trail they'd half-slid down. There was no way of knowing, of course, if Cele had started down this particular trail before her fatal fall, or if she'd fallen (or jumped or was pushed) from the very top of the cliffs. The evidence there just wasn't clear. Or perhaps she'd had no intention that day of climbing down to the shore. The possibilities were many. They'd have to examine each and every one, discarding and amplifying as they went, to see which might actually stick. In many ways, this was the most complex case they'd ever tackled, and there was no certainty they'd ever be able to solve it. Still, here they were, on this gorgeous California day, and for now, they were the smartest people in the room.

Meanwhile, Charles and Mr. Maleta were having a quiet discussion about the vagaries of life. The old man seemed insistent on outlining the perils of Karma, specifically how his understanding of the concept might relate to the question at hand. Charles, a straightforward, no-nonsense kind of guy, could not see for the life of him how any of this would throw light on the mystery of Cele's death, but he was a kind and considerate person at heart, and decided to just 'go with the flow' of Mr. Maleta's pronouncements, and see where it might lead him.

'But . . . ' Charles was saying now, 'I don't see how *you* could possibly know that Karma played a hand in her death. I mean, it *might* have, sure, but *how would you know that?*'

'All things must be related. All life . . . all death. When you fell down the cliff, how did it begin? Do you recall?'

'Hmm. Well, I guess I just took a wrong step — '

'Exactly, you took a *wrong* step! It was not intentional, but all the same, *you took that wrong step* . . . and set in motion the whole earth beneath your feet! Do you not see?'

'Yes . . . I suppose,' Charles said uncertainly, 'but I didn't mean to do it. I thought Karma was when you did something — to someone else — intentionally. For good or evil, I mean. If you do something good, then good will return to you. If you do something evil, then evil, most certainly, will come back on you. Am I wrong?'

'The key principle is the action itself. Sometimes we do things without thinking about it, without planning to do it. Something happens and we react. It makes no difference if you planned to do it. The action itself will set the rest of the story in motion. Just as the step you took brought you and your friends to me. I might have been away from the house. I might not have seen or heard you call out as you fell. You, like the young woman, might very well have died — down there, alone. Do you see?'

'And you most certainly *would* have gone to her aid if you had seen her fall.'

'Yes — but then you and I would never have met. We would not be sitting here together now — under this tree — drinking this lemonade, enjoying this beautiful day together. You see how the mosaic of life changes constantly — ever adjusting, ever adapting, to each and every little nuance? What caused you and your friends to become so interested in this case?' Maleta's bright black eyes, like shoe buttons, showed amusement at Charles's struggle to understand what, to him, was a very basic philosophy.

'I think I'm beginning to understand — a little,' Charles paused and looked out over the yard, the trees. The first time he saw this place he thought it was ugly and unkempt. Now he saw only beauty, light, even peace. 'Each thing that happens, or that we cause to happen, results in something occurring on the other side of it. Like hitting a ball against the side of a house, I suppose. If you hit it correctly, square on, it will come right back to you. If you hit it to one side, then it might go off somewhere into the dirt or the mud. You might lose it and never find it again ... I suppose that's how Nick must feel about his relationship with Cele. One wrong move and she was lost to him forever. If he had known the *right* move to make, she might not have come here, might still be alive.'

'You are beginning to see, I think. Keep working on it. One day it will all come clear. Now — where are these pictures? I am most anxious to assist you in your investigation. I will make the utmost effort, my friend, to stretch and pull my memory as far as it will go. I pray now that I will be able to make a difference for you.'

'You already *have* made a difference — at least to me. Here, this is the photograph of the woman. Take your time. Don't rush. We have all the time in the world.'

* * *

'Where is that little map *you* drew, Connie — the one we gleaned from that

201

report Charles got from the coroner's office?' Hugo was spreading the maps out on top of the big flat rock that they had now pressed to become a worktable of sorts. 'I need to get my bearings better.'

'Here it is,' Connie pointed to the sheet he'd painstakingly constructed the night before. 'I tried to be as accurate as possible. They mentioned several of the nearby landmarks, including this rock. See . . . '

'Yes, I think you're right. Now, if we step off in this direction . . . ' Hugo, counting as he went, headed down the beach toward another section of the nearly vertical cliffs jutting up from the sand. Nick was close on his heels, carrying the collapsible shovel, followed by Connie with the rope. This time Gail brought up the rear, holding her little camera close to protect it from the powerful salt spray. 'Here!' Hugo called finally, as he drew to a halt. 'I think this is where they had to climb up to the body.'

They paused to gaze upward about ten feet towards a cleft in the rock. Gail put a comforting hand on Nick's shoulder. She could sense the warring emotions in him — apprehension at finally seeing the spot where Cele had died — and relief that he was now in a position to make amends to the ghost that still haunted him.

'All right,' she said. 'Let's see what we can make of this.'

★ ★ ★

A few days later, Gail called the number Timmy Lerner had provided. After leaving a message on his voice-mail, she made a second call — this time to Bobby Burrell, Jr. 'Mr. Burrell? I don't know if you recall speaking with me earlier, but this is Gail Brevard. I have some information about Cele's death that I'd like to share with you. Could you join me and a few of my friends for drinks this evening about eight? Fine. My suite is at the Nob Hill Hotel in San Francisco. We'll be expecting you.'

As she hung up, she caught the tail end of Connie's conversation with Wicks. 'Yes. I thought you'd like to be in on this. I've contacted both Detective Ramírez and

Deputy Singleton as well. They'll be 'on call,' so to speak, in the next room. I think you'll find this all very interesting.'

After an early supper, Connie, Gail, Nick, and Charles gathered in the suite to talk strategy. Everything depended on Gail's interrogation skills and Connie's meticulous planning. Hugo had made the rounds of the suite, setting up his unobtrusive cameras and microphones, making sure everything could be seen and heard without difficulty in the adjoining bedroom. Finally, about 6:30 or so, the two detectives and their teams, all in plain clothes, appeared and received their final briefing. Everyone took their places, then sat back to wait.

The first arrival was Bob Burrell. He gave a cursory nod to Nick, but if he was surprised to see his former co-worker in attendance, he chose not to show it. The waiter standing by (who was actually one of Ramírez's men in disguise) took the newcomer's drink order and retired to the room bar to prepare it. Conversation was polite and desultory. Burrell seemed curious about why he was there, but asked no questions.

Wicks showed up right after Bob. He and Connie made for the bar where they had a quiet discussion, Johnnie nodding his head furiously at everything Connie said.

Just as Gail was beginning to think they'd planned all this in vain, the buzzer rang once more. The waiter opened the door to reveal Timmy Lerner and, behind him, an older couple, clearly related to him, and a younger woman in uniform cuddling a tiny infant protectively in her arms. The man had a striking full head of white hair.

Gail and Connie hurried forward. 'Mr. Lerner, Timmy! How nice to see you again. This is my partner, Conrad Osterlitz. These are your parents, Mr. and Mrs. Lerner? Please come in. Is this the baby and his nanny? He's darling . . . '
Gail babbled on, urging her reluctant guests into the room, getting everyone settled, and sending the waiter around to take their drink orders. She told the nanny that she'd rented the room next door, and had set up a crib and other

facilities there — and the nurse gratefully departed with the baby.

Gail couldn't help but notice the icy stares between Burrell and the Lerners, and took care to seat them well apart. Connie, bless his heart, immediately drew the elder Lerner into a detailed discussion about the latter's profession which, interestingly enough, included a long stint as a property developer in the Carmonte area. Charles, meantime, got Burrell going on about the vagaries of the real estate business in Tucson. Nick, with his wide experience in the City, drew Mrs. Lerner into a conversation about her life as a society matron in the Bay Area, her favorite shops, the service organizations she frequented, and the like.

Once she was certain everyone was relaxed and occupied, Gail approached Timmy again, and said in a loud voice that carried throughout the room: 'You know, there's one thing that has just been bugging me. Do you have any idea why Cele wandered out to the cliffs that day? It seems so unlike her. I mean . . . ' She paused to take a sip of her wine in an offhand manner. 'I mean, she was notorious for being clumsy, wasn't she? At least she was in school. I don't know how many spills she took, running up and down steps, getting in and out of cars. You know, there was one time — it almost makes me laugh to think of it — except, of course . . . well, this one time, she'd cooked a meal for several of her friends, all on her own, which was unusual in itself . . . ' She was babbling now, but out of the corner of her eye she could tell Timmy was growing more and more agitated as she spoke. 'Anyway, she decided, for what reason we could never figure out, that she was going to cook a goose! An actual goose! And she'd never fixed one before. Well, wouldn't you know — she had everything all ready, the table all set, and as she took it out of the oven and started to carry it in to the dining room . . . WHOOM . . . ' Everyone in the room looked up, startled by the exclamation. Now she had their complete attention. ' . . . Whoom! The whole thing, Goose, gravy and all, went sliding to the floor. It was a complete disaster!' Gail

stopped suddenly and looked James
Lerner in the eye.

'Perhaps *you* can tell us, Mr. Lerner.
Why would someone so clumsy — who
knew she was clumsy — walk out along
the cliffs in such a treacherous spot
— without having someone with her?
Someone she trusted? Someone who
could have rescued her if she fell? *Why,*
Mr. Lerner? Could it be that someone
she knew had asked her there? To show
her a piece of property where a
beautiful home would be built one day
— for his son and daughter-in-law and
their new baby?'

'What are you talking about? Why are
you saying this?' Timmy grabbed at Gail's
arm in consternation. Connie stepped
forward, but Gail held up her hand.

'Please, Mr. Lerner, we're waiting for
an answer.'

'I don't know what you mean, young
woman,' the elder Lerner snapped. 'I
know of no such plans in the works. I was
nowhere near the cliffs that day . . . my
wife can vouch for me.'

Mrs. Lerner looked dazed, but nodded

her head in assent. 'Whatever he says . . . ' she murmured, 'whatever he says is true.'

'Charles?' Gail waved to him across the room where he and Burrell were quietly observing the fireworks.

'Yes.' He stepped forward, a sheaf of papers in his hand. 'Mr. Lerner, The Santa Lucia County deed records show that one James Allen Lerner, *you*, sir, are the sole owner of a ten-acre plot of land overlooking the ocean in the Cliffside area. This property was deeded to you in settlement of an unpaid loan you'd made to a fisherman by the name of Dario Maleta, over forty years ago. The man fell on hard times, and rather than allowing him to work out the debt, *as any decent person would have done*, you foreclosed on the property, thus pushing him into a life of poverty. He was only allowed to lease a tiny, quarter-acre lot and an old hut. There he resided, and still resides, making what living he can from the sea and his garden.

'The ten acres, on the other hand, were allowed to lie fallow all these years, because you had no desire to live there yourself, and you were too greedy to give it up. Your greatest hope was that the Carmonte community would eventually expand south into that area — thus allowing you to make a killing.' Charles grimaced at the unintended pun.

'Recently, your only son and heir, James Timothy Lerner, *Jr.*, known from his school days as Timmy, married a young woman from a family that you and your wife felt were beneath your standards socially. Try as you might, you could not break the marriage. You even went so far as to spread rumors about the young woman in question, hoping to discredit her in Timmy's eyes. While this led to frequent arguments between the couple, they failed to separate. Then a child was born, a baby son. The birth was difficult and your daughter-in-law was warned that she would probably never carry another child to term. Your wife was enthralled with the new baby, and determined to have as much influence over the raising of the infant as possible. Still, your son's wife was stubborn. In spite of all your manipulations and scheming, she hung on, determined to make her marriage work.' Charles looked back to Gail.

'It doesn't take much imagination to envision a scenario where you called your daughter-in-law for a heart-to-heart.' She picked up the thread. 'At the meeting, you informed her of the 'beautiful beach property' you owned in Santa Lucia County, and how it was your intention, in honor of the new grandchild, to build a brand new home on this site, all as a surprise for your son. It was *you*, wasn't it, Mr. Lerner, who suggested that she arrange to leave her home 'for just a few days,' meet you at the Cliffside Lodge, and go with you to inspect the site of the proposed new home? And it was *you* who argued with Cele Burrell at the side of the cliff and, in a fit of anger, it was *you* who pushed her over the edge, *wasn't it*?'

'Why . . . even if that were true, which it isn't, I don't see how you can prove it,' Lerner sputtered, gesturing and knocking the drink off the table at his side.

'Oh, but I can . . . and I will,' Gail said

triumphantly, pointing to the bedroom door. There, in the shadowed room beyond, stood Mr. Maleta, a shaking finger pointing directly at James Lerner, Sr.

'Yes, that is him. *That* is most certainly the 'light-haired' man I saw on the cliffs that day, arguing with that poor young lady, the one in the picture you showed me,' he looked at Charles in triumph. 'You see! I told you it was karma! It was karma all the time!'

Lerner looked around the room, and finally shook his head, and with a sneer exhaled one small laugh. 'You'll never establish that in court, counselor, as you well know.'

'Perhaps,' she said, 'but the bad publicity will ruin you, and give other folks the courage to take action. I have no doubt that there are plenty of other things you've done that'll emerge from the shadows.'

The waters parted, and Detective Ramírez and Deputy Singleton strode forward to read James Lerner, Sr. his rights.

Timmy Lerner rushed to his mother's side. 'We'll get an attorney, Mother, right away. We won't allow them to do this to us . . .'

As Lerner, Sr. was led off, Wicks made a quick call to his office to literally 'stop the presses' for a big story. He winked at Connie as he spoke and gave a thumbs-up for 'job well done.' This would be huge, and the resulting trial would probably take months, if not years. Johnnie smiled happily, clearly in his element.

'Now,' said Gail to Connie, 'now for the hard part.'

She led the way over to Nick, standing on the sidelines, listening to the bits and pieces of conversation whirring about him. 'We have to talk — in private,' she said. She nodded at Charles, who was eyeing them apprehensively, then directed Nick to the bedroom. Hugo, with the help of some of the officers, was clearing out the remainder of the listening equipment. The big overhead light had been switched on, and the room enveloped them like a cocoon. Once the three were alone, she began again.

'There's something else we have to discuss. It might mean nothing — or it might mean everything. When you told us you hadn't seen Cele for a while before her marriage — what did you mean by 'a while?' '

Nick looked confused for a moment then a series of raw emotions flickered across his face. 'I saw her for the last time just a month before her marriage. We'd decided to make an end of it. We were obviously moving in opposite directions. She couldn't understand why I wanted . . . why I *had* to leave her family's firm. I couldn't understand why *she* couldn't understand. It was hopeless.'

'Now, you don't have to answer this, of course, but were you intimate that last time? Did you have relations with her?'

'Why . . . ? Why would you . . . ?' he paused, light dawning on his tortured face. 'Oh God, you don't mean . . . ? How . . . ? I thought she was taking precautions . . . ' He turned away from them in anguish.

'The baby's full name is Timothy Nicholas Lerner. Cele insisted on that name . . . and the intention was to call him 'Nicholas.' I got a good look at him, in the nanny's arms. There's little doubt in *my* mind. But a DNA test would set everything straight. That is, if you want to pursue this. Connie and I will help you, but it's your decision. I'm not at all sure Mrs. Lerner would still be interested in the baby, if she knew the truth of the matter. I'm reasonably sure Timmy doesn't suspect, no reason for him to, unless Cele told him in a fit of anger. Somehow I don't think she did. But I do think it was what she was so desperate to talk to *you* about. Well, like I said, the decision is yours.'

'I'll — I'll need to think about it a bit. But I'll probably follow through on this, for Cele's sake, as well as mine — and Nicholas's.' Nick shook his head. 'Man, you just never know, do you, how a simple act of love will turn out.'

Mr. Maleta, looking in from the doorway, smiled at him, and shook his head slightly.

'Oh, if only they understood,' he said to himself.

THE END

We do hope that you have enjoyed reading this large print book.

Did you know that all of our titles are available for purchase?

We publish a wide range of high quality large print books including:
Romances, Mysteries, Classics
General Fiction
Non Fiction and Westerns

Special interest titles available in large print are:
The Little Oxford Dictionary
Music Book, Song Book
Hymn Book, Service Book

Also available from us courtesy of Oxford University Press:
Young Readers' Dictionary
(large print edition)
Young Readers' Thesaurus
(large print edition)

For further information or a free brochure, please contact us at:
Ulverscroft Large Print Books Ltd.,
The Green, Bradgate Road, Anstey,
Leicester, LE7 7FU, England.
Tel: (00 44) 0116 236 4325
Fax: (00 44) 0116 234 0205

Other titles in the
Linford Mystery Library:

VICTORIAN VILLAINY

Michael Kurland

Professor James Moriarty stands alone as the particular nemesis of Sherlock Holmes. But just how evil was he? Here are four ingenious stories, all exploring an alternate possibility: that Moriarty wasn't really a villain at all. But why, then, did Holmes describe Moriarty as 'the greatest schemer of all time', and 'the Napoleon of crime'? Holmes could never *catch* Moriarty in any of his imagined schemes — which only reinforced his conviction that the professor was, indeed, an evil genius . . .